THE PROCTOR HALL HORROR

The Bayou Hauntings
Book Seven

Bill Thompson

Published by
Ascendente Books
Dallas, Texas

This is a work of fiction. Where real people, events, businesses, organizations and locales appear, they are used fictitiously. All other elements of this novel are products of the author's imagination. The author has represented and warranted full ownership and/or legal rights to publish all the materials in this book.

The Proctor Hall Horror: The Bayou Hauntings 7
All Rights Reserved
Copyright © 2020
V.1.0
This book may not be reproduced, transmitted or stored in whole or in part by any means, including graphic, electronic or mechanical without the express written consent of the author except in the case of brief quotations embodied in critical articles and reviews.

Published by Ascendente Books
ISBN 978-09992503-8-9
Printed in the United States of America

Books by Bill Thompson

<u>The Bayou Hauntings</u>
CALLIE
FORGOTTEN MEN
THE NURSERY
BILLY WHISTLER
THE EXPERIMENTS
DIE AGAIN
THE PROCTOR HALL HORROR

<u>Brian Sadler Archaeological Mystery Series</u>
THE BETHLEHEM SCROLL
ANCIENT: A SEARCH FOR THE LOST CITY OF THE MAYAS
THE STRANGEST THING
THE BONES IN THE PIT
ORDER OF SUCCESSION
THE BLACK CROSS
TEMPLE

<u>Apocalyptic Fiction</u>
THE OUTCASTS

<u>The Crypt Trilogy</u>
THE RELIC OF THE KING
THE CRYPT OF THE ANCIENTS
GHOST TRAIN

<u>Middle Grade Fiction</u>
THE LEGEND OF GUNNERS COVE

When my boys were little, I often read ghost stories to them, but they loved it most when I created spooky tales of my own. I'd describe the haunted cabin by a lake, or the lady in white that floated past the window of the old house in our town.

*I dedicate this ghost story to other parents who have told made-up stories to their own kids,
who encourage them to read and learn,
and who love a good scary story as much as I do.*

Significant Characters in The Proctor Hall Horror

LANDRY DRAKE
Paranormal ghost hunter and creator of the nationally popular *Bayou Hauntings* television series. Works for WCCY-TV Channel Nine in New Orleans

CATE ADAMS
Landry's girlfriend who works for Henri Duchamp

DOC ADAMS
Cate's father, a prominent psychiatrist in Galveston who invests in distressed properties

HENRI DUCHAMP
President of Louisiana Society for the Paranormal. Old friend of Landry's who works closely with him on cases.

MARGUEY SLATTERY
Teenaged girl who vanished at Proctor Hall

THE PROCTORS
Hiram, Sarah and May Ellen were victims of the Proctor Hall Massacre in 1963. Son Noah was blamed for killing his father, mother and sister.

THE TRIMBLES
Ben was caretaker of Proctor Hall before and after the massacre. Agnes is his common-law wife.

THE GIRARDS
Joseph and Mary are relatives of the Trimbles.

DR. JULIEN GIRARD
History professor at Tulane University and creator of a course in Louisiana culture

HARRY KANTER
State police lieutenant who works regularly on cases with Landry

SHANE YOUNG
New Orleans police detective who works regularly on cases with Landry

CHAPTER ONE

Wind whipped through the ancient live oaks that hung low over Bayou Lafourche. The sky turned a deep purple as ominous clouds swept over the parish. The weatherman had predicted thunderstorms around four p.m., and his forecast was right on the money. Fat drops fell, slowly at first, then increasing in speed and intensity until the heavens opened up.

Marguey Slattery poled her pirogue toward the bank. Two hours ago when she put in, the weather had been perfect. Her dad had warned her to be back by three, but she'd lost track of time as she floated past the old plantation homes that fronted the bayou. Now it was too late — she'd have to ride out the storm under one of the massive old oaks.

She dug the pole into the bottom, turning the pirogue to reach a branch and tie off. Marguey wasn't certain where she was. Some distance from the river stood a house she hadn't seen before. Even in the gloom, no lights shone in the windows. The house looked abandoned.

BILL THOMPSON

Daddy's gonna be mad. I'm gonna get the lecture of my life. Maybe even a whipping.

Just a few miles from home, she might have tried going back, but she couldn't risk it in the powerful rainstorm.

Better for Daddy to be mad than for me to drown in the bayou.

More drenched by the minute, Marguey sat in the pirogue and pulled her straw hat down low. It did little more than filter the raindrops, but that helped. She looked at the old house again and thought she saw something. Was someone standing on the lawn? She dug out the binoculars she'd brought along for bird-watching, wiped down the lenses, and looked.

She *did* see someone. A child younger than Marguey in a black dress stood in the yard. There was a hood over her head so she wouldn't get wet. She raised her hand.

She's — she's waving at me! How does she know I'm here, as dark as it is here in these trees? Is someone really there?

Marguey stopped to clear the lenses again and looked. Now the girl stood halfway down the yard, standing between the house and the pirogue.

How did she move that quickly?

Her face was hidden by the hood, but the howling wind made a sound like words. She beckoned to Marguey, and the wind said, "Come play with me."

This is crazy! She's out in the pouring rain but doesn't seem to notice. Who is she? What's going on?

Marguey shouted, "I can't come up there. It's storming!"

THE PROCTOR HALL HORROR

The binoculars fell onto the floor of the pirogue. Marguey strained to get them, and when she sat upright again, she cried out.

The girl stood on the bank not three feet away, her face dark inside the hood. She — or perhaps the wind — said, "Come play with me."

Marguey fumbled with the rope, trying to untie it. Being out on the bayou in a storm was a lot less scary than being right here. As she fumbled with the knot, the girl moved again. Now they were close enough to touch each other. A sudden, powerful gust of wind blew the girl's hood back, and Marguey realized that tying off here had been a huge mistake.

The figure standing in front of her had no head.

The wind spoke. "Don't leave. I want you to play with me."

CHAPTER TWO

"What's the most haunted plantation home in Louisiana?"

All sixteen students raised their hands, and Julien Girard said, "Camilla, let's hear your choice."

"The Myrtles in St. Francisville."

"A logical choice," Dr. Girard said, asking the class who agreed with her. As usual, the vast majority chose it too. Only three had other ideas.

Oak Alley. Chretien Point. San Francisco Plantation.

They always pick the same ones. "You've made four excellent choices, but the title 'most haunted' depends on who you ask. Every Louisianan has an opinion, and if you ask a hundred people, you'll get a variety of answers.

"Here's my idea. The most haunted plantation house in Louisiana is Proctor Hall in Lafourche Parish. Not many people know about it."

BILL THOMPSON

He flashed a picture on a screen. "As you can see, it's not a beautiful old mansion like the ones you just mentioned. It's a farmhouse on a plantation along Bayou Lafourche.

"Proctor Hall was the scene of one of the most grisly mass murders in the twentieth century and the most horrific ever in that parish. Here's your assignment for the weekend. Research the story, find out as much as you can about what happened there, and turn in a report on Monday. There's more to the story of Proctor Hall than you might expect, so the top grades go to those of you who dig the deepest. We'll discuss it then."

As the students filed out of Julien Girard's classroom on the third floor of Tulane's Hebert Hall, he considered which of them would do the minimum on this project and who would really embrace it. There was plenty about what the press dubbed the Massacre at Proctor Hall, but almost nothing about the other eerie things that had happened there over the years. The only A's for this assignment would go to those who learned more than the obvious.

After teaching history for twenty-eight years, Julien knew almost every tall tale and spooky story there was. But when he created a course called Appreciation of Louisiana Culture, he'd found his true calling. For the past three years he'd been enchanting his students with the legends of Cajun country. Julien was a master storyteller, and every semester there was a waiting list of people who wanted to take his course. His rugged good looks and black hair pulled back into a ponytail didn't hurt his popularity with the coeds either.

The part of his job he loved most was preparing his curriculum for the next semester. He spent summers driving the back roads of southwestern Louisiana, exploring old houses and hearing about mysteries and ghosts. In town after town, he listened to stories from ordinary people who claimed to have witnessed

THE PROCTOR HALL HORROR

unexplainable events. All that research ended up as fodder for his students to ponder.

Although it had happened a few years before he was born, Julien knew every detail about the Massacre at Proctor Hall. It fascinated him to watch his students dig into the mysteries there. Would they turn up all the secrets the old house held? Not a chance. Nobody ever did, because they'd been so well concealed all these years.

On Monday morning, his students drifted back into the classroom. He could tell from the looks on their faces who had enjoyed working on Friday's assignment and who gave it the usual "just enough to get by" effort.

"I hope everyone had a great weekend," he began. "And I hope you found researching Proctor Hall intriguing. It's one of my favorite stories. Is there anyone who didn't do the assignment? Dog ate my homework? I had the flu? My mother grounded me and I couldn't use the computer?"

Everyone laughed, but no one raised a hand. That was always gratifying. At least they all tried.

"Who thinks their research is best? Who among you thinks you'll get the top grade today?"

One hand shot up before he'd finished the first question — Marisol de Leon's. No surprise there. Over the years, a variety of students had passed through his classroom and his life. Underachievers, overachievers, those who struggled, the cocky, the shy, those who loved his subject, and those who took it to fill an elective and graduate.

Marisol had a classic type A personality — driven, ambitious, ruthless and determined to be best at whatever she did. Naturally she'd consider her work the best. And it probably was, but he had to be fair to the class.

BILL THOMPSON

"Okay, Marisol, we'll save the best for last." He and she laughed, but the others didn't. Early in the semester they had tired of her ego trips. By now it was fifteen against one — the class against the beautiful, sultry senior from southern California.

"How about you, Andy?" Girard asked, looking at the only other senior in his class. Andy Arnaud slouched in his chair, chewing on a toothpick and exhibiting his trademark "don't give a shit" attitude.

Andy was one of those who did just enough to get by. He was here for one reason. His parents wanted him to have a degree. Andy couldn't care less because he wouldn't be job hunting after he walked across the stage. His father owned a dozen car dealerships across the state. Andy's folks were what wealthy people in the deep South called "new money." It wasn't a flattering term.

"I looked it up like you said," the boy replied. "Old house, kid kills his whole family, he's nuts so they can't fry his ass, yada yada yada. That's the ten-second version of Proctor Hall."

"If minimizing the horrors of Proctor Hall had been the assignment, you'd be the winner for sure," Julien snapped, but why get angry? Andy wouldn't change, and he wasn't worth the effort.

He listened to summaries from a few more before asking the big question. "How many of you came across the name Marguey Slattery?"

Eight hands went up, Marisol's first and highest. Half the class.

"Okay. Now here's a question for those who *didn't* come across Marguey's name. Don't yell out the answer. Raise your hands. Who killed the three members of the Proctor family in 1963?"

As he had expected, all eight students raised their hands. And six out of eight fell for the trick question, just like they did every semester.

Six said, "Noah Proctor."

Julien asked the other two, "If Noah didn't do it, who did?"

"Nobody knows who killed the family," they said, and they were right.

Julien said, "Six of you answered as most people would, but the facts are clear. Noah was never charged and never convicted. You drew a conclusion from an improper basic premise. If everything else in the report you turn in is right, I'll give you a C, but that's the best you can hope for."

At last he called on Marisol. "You think your report's the best. Tell us the story of Proctor Hall."

CHAPTER THREE

With confidence and a hint of smugness, Marisol walked to the lectern. *She'll be addressing groups for the rest of her life,* Julien thought as he watched her arrange her notes and prepare to speak. *This one will be a CEO or own a hedge fund or be President of the United States.*

She arranged her notes and began. Little online information existed about Proctor Hall or the family prior to 1963. Mason Proctor emigrated from somewhere up north to Lafourche Parish in the first decade of the twentieth century. He bought a thousand acres of land on the bayou and built a home in the Queen Anne Revival style in 1910 that became known as Proctor Hall.

Mason's only child, Hiram, was born at the house in 1928. From the scant information available, Marisol assumed Hiram took over the sugarcane operation from his father. He married Susan Proctor, and they had two children, Noah in 1949 and May Ellen in 1954. Perhaps autistic, Noah never spoke.

According to news stories and the sheriff's report Marisol found, one bright Sunday morning in 1963, a man named

BILL THOMPSON

Mike, the plantation supervisor, came to the house to check on his boss. Mr. Proctor had missed the daily meeting with the field hands. It was a rare thing, and Mike wondered if things were okay.

The front door stood open, and Mike knocked on the frame and looked inside. On a stairway near the entrance sat fourteen-year-old Noah covered in blood. Mike yelled at Noah and asked what happened. The boy never changed expression or moved or seemed to realize Mike was there. He just stared off into space somewhere.

When he went inside, Mike saw crimson footprints heading down a hallway. He glanced at Noah's bloodstained shoes and walked gingerly down the hall, avoiding stepping on the prints but following them into a sitting room.

The only sound in the classroom was Marisol's voice, and Professor Girard was as enthralled by the story as the kids. No matter how many times he heard it, the Proctor Hall story always gave him goosebumps.

Marisol read the Baton Rouge *Advocate*'s account of what the supervisor found. The caretaker's eyewitness account was chilling. "If there had been people besides Noah within a mile of me, my shrieks would have scared the hell out of them. I found the rest of the family — old man Proctor; his wife, Susan; and their twelve-year-old daughter, May Ellen — all sitting on the couch. Noah had propped them up with pillows. With one exception, they just sat there as if waiting for you to come in and join them for a chat."

That exception was that their heads rested on the mantel above the fireplace.

CHAPTER FOUR

Marisol continued. Soon the farmhouse buzzed with activity. Parish and state officers combed the place room by room while two detectives sat in the kitchen, trying to interview Noah, who neither looked at them nor spoke. Mike the supervisor said the kid didn't talk, but it surprised deputies that at age fourteen he displayed no emotion about the deaths of his family.

One officer commented either he was the coldest person on earth or downright crazy. His mother, father and sister sat in the next room, decapitated, but Noah's demeanor never changed one iota. The cops even took him into the parlor where the bodies sat. He saw them — they held his head and forced him to look — but he showed neither understanding nor concern about what he'd done.

The supervisor said a man named Ben Trimble had been old man Proctor's handyman for several years. Off on Sundays, the deputies found him at home in Thibodaux. Twenty-five-year-old Ben lived with his common-law wife in a dilapidated shotgun house near the bayou. He said they had been at church all morning. Shocked to learn about the murders, he told police he always knew Noah "wasn't right in the head" and that something awful might happen. And no, the family didn't fight or bicker. There wasn't any love either — just coexistence in that big old house.

He added that the dead Proctor girl, May Ellen, attended Catholic school in town, but Noah hadn't gone since first grade. His teacher claimed he couldn't learn anything, and Noah's father and mother gave up on him. The caretaker said Noah just sat on the stairs every day, lost in another world. His mother would go get him at mealtimes, and he even pissed in his pants sometimes when she forgot to tell him to use the restroom. Trimble described him as a boy whose mind was a locked room with no key.

Even without witnesses, what happened seemed indisputable. The demented boy killed his parents, hid the murder weapon somewhere, and refused to tell investigators what happened. It was a Sunday and they had no place to take Noah for the night except to the parish jail. Given his age and apparent mental incapacity, they stuck him in a holding cell away from the other prisoners. The next day a judge would determine his future.

Children and Family Services professionals evaluated Noah and determined he couldn't stand trial either as a juvenile or an adult. His mental acuity was above average — a surprise to those who considered him impaired — so he either chose never to speak or he couldn't. He expressed no emotion, and his demeanor never changed. He initiated nothing on his own; even changing clothes happened only when a worker handed him fresh clothing and told him to put them on. The doctors said he couldn't defend himself. That and a lack of witnesses meant no one was ever charged with the brutal murders of his family.

They sent Noah to an institution for further evaluation, and there he remained for many years. At first the doctors spent a lot of time with the mute boy, but at some point they gave up. Regardless of what therapies or processes they tried,

THE PROCTOR HALL HORROR

nothing ever changed, and after a few years he became lost in the system. With no one to champion his cause, he sat in a locked room. Every day an orderly took him outside for an hour in the sun, to his meals and the recreation room. Noah would stare at the television, seeing it but not really watching.

Julien's head jerked up as the bell rang. The time had flown as he listened once again to the fascinating account of Proctor Hall, but now class was over.

"We'll continue this saga on Wednesday," he said to a rare chorus of groans. Usually students left quickly, but today they wanted more.

The kids begged Marisol to continue — which was a big deal since no one liked her. She didn't have another class after this, and the students asked Julien if she could continue. In the end, even those with back-to-back classes skipped the next one, which pleased Marisol.

She continued, "I found several articles about what happened to Noah. It surprised me that one of the most thorough and entertaining appeared in a 1991 issue of *Reader's Digest*."

Julien nodded; he'd also found that one interesting.

In 1989, twenty-six years after the deaths of his family members, Noah was deemed fit to return to society. There had been no miraculous recovery. They decided to release him based on two things. One was the forty thousand dollars a year it cost to keep him in a state facility. And also he never created a problem, never exhibiting violent or disruptive tendencies. Quite the opposite — he never spoke or did anything proactive. A psychiatrist signed his release papers, saying Noah Proctor posed no danger to society or himself. He wasn't "cured," but he was free.

BILL THOMPSON

Although the facility was in essence abandoning him, his doctor knew this patient must have someplace to go and people to care for him. A typical forty-year-old patient would walk out the door and re-enter the world, but this man was different. He would require help for the rest of his life.

The basic problem was that he had no one to go home to. He had murdered and decapitated his only relatives. The director of the hospital called the Lafourche Parish sheriff for advice, and the sheriff went to Proctor Hall to see if anyone was still there. He found the caretaker and his wife, Ben and Agnes Trimble, living in the house.

Trimble told the sheriff he'd moved in after the Proctors died. With no family to take care of the property, he'd stayed on to keep the house up. The plantation was another story. With no one to pay the workers, the sugarcane operation shut down, and the workers moved on. The roof on the huge old sugar mill collapsed, leaving four tall brick walls and a lot of ruined machinery. Many wooden outbuildings still stood — the barns, barracks, offices, blacksmith shop and so forth — but they were left to the elements. By leasing the land to the sugar cooperative, Ben had sufficient income to pay for upkeep.

The sheriff noticed the place needed fixing up, but Trimble at least tried to keep his old employer's house and land from ruin. Technically the couple were squatters, but the sheriff saw no reason to challenge their living at Proctor Hall.

To the lawman's surprise, Ben said they could bring Noah back to Proctor Hall. He and Agnes would care for the man. It was proper that he live here despite his horrible crimes, Ben said. It was his home, even though he'd been gone for more than half his life.

THE PROCTOR HALL HORROR

"The doctors say he's no danger to himself or others," the sheriff advised, and Ben said it was nothing to worry about. He wasn't afraid of Noah. Hell, he'd known him since he was a kid. He did some awful things a long time ago, but they wouldn't have a problem with him.

You two are as strange as Noah, the sheriff thought, but he let it go. Thanks to Ben Trimble, Noah had a place to come home to. Done deal and potential problem solved. Four days later, a deputy brought Noah back to Proctor Hall.

According to the *Reader's Digest* article, that was when all the strange things started. Nocturnal things that fishermen on Bayou Lafourche saw in the wee hours. Ghostly specters floated on the porches and the grounds, eerie lights flickered in the upstairs windows, and unearthly shrieks scared even the bravest of them.

Then there were the legends — the folktales about uncanny things at the old house. On the anniversary night of the massacre, daring teens and even adults crept up to the old house and witnessed horrifying things that scared them out of their wits.

"I heard moans and groans coming from somewhere inside," one said. "I peeked in a window. It was the sitting room where they died. Fresh blood was dripping from the mantel, and a bloody machete lay on the floor by the couch. I sensed something behind me — a dark thing that floated in the air — and I ran for my life. I'll never go back there again as long as I live. Those who do never come out."

Those unproven stories proliferated among the residents of Lafourche Parish. They were ghost stories that added to the mystery and eeriness of the house, and they kept most people away from Proctor Hall.

Marisol said, "We know some things about the house, but not everything. So many questions remain unanswered.

How did Noah kill one of them after another without somebody resisting and stopping him? What was the murder weapon? The police said maybe it was an ax, but they never found it. There's no record of what happened to the bodies of the victims — or their heads. There were no funerals, so where are the Proctors buried?"

That was the end of her report on the massacre, and she switched to the 1998 disappearance of Marguey Slattery. It was yet another unsolved mystery involving Proctor Hall. By then Noah was back home, so was Marguey another of his victims?

The professor said, "We're out of time, so let's leave Marguey for now. You did a great job uncovering a fascinating story, Marisol. Thanks to the rest of you for staying to hear it. See you Wednesday."

CHAPTER FIVE

One evening last winter Julien and two other Tulane professors had met in a Freret Street bar. He asked if either had any haunted house stories for his fall course on Louisiana culture, and someone mentioned the Marguey Slattery disappearance. The tale had garnered local attention, but the man talking was from Thibodaux, and he had heard a lot more than the media reported.

"Everyone knows about the Massacre at Proctor Hall, where the kid cut the heads off his entire family back in the sixties, but Marguey's a different story."

Julien said, "She disappeared somewhere down on Bayou Lafourche twenty years or so ago, as I recall."

"She disappeared at Proctor Hall."

Keen to learn his friend's story, Julien listened to a mixture of fact, gossip and theories. It went like this — fourteen-year-old Marguey Slattery was in her pirogue on Bayou Lafourche one afternoon. When a thundershower popped up, she pulled under a tree along the bank to wait it out.

Hours later when she hadn't returned home, her father, Emile, went looking for her in a bass boat.

"Her dad said he shuddered when he found the pirogue tied up on the bank and looked off in the distance. There stood Proctor Hall.

"Emile Slattery was a friend of my mother's," the tale-teller continued. "Plus, the Massacre at Proctor Hall was the biggest crime that ever happened in the parish. People steered clear of the old house, and Marguey's dad never understood why his daughter picked that place to hunker down. It spooked him to walk to the house, but he was desperate. He hoped to God she ran to the house to get out of the rain, and she got hurt or something. It was far-fetched, but it gave him hope.

"Emile became frantic when he saw her straw hat lying on the porch. He banged on the door, and the caretaker, a man named Ben Trimble, who answered said no girl had come around. Marguey's father shoved him aside and ran into the entry hall, shouting her name.

"He trembled when he saw Noah Proctor sitting on the stairway a few feet away. 'Where's my daughter? What have you done with her?' he yelled. And of course Noah said nothing. The caretaker grabbed Emile, wrestled him out onto the front porch, and ordered him off the property.

"'We ain't seen your daughter and the boy has nothing to do with it,' he yelled. That's when Marguey's father called the sheriff.

"The authorities searched the house, but nothing indicated the girl had ever been there. Naturally the cops suspected Noah, but with no evidence except a straw hat on the porch, they left.

THE PROCTOR HALL HORROR

"That was eighteen years ago. Marguey Slattery would be thirty-two now. Her daddy died a few years after her disappearance, some said of a broken heart. He spent the remaining years of his life warning others to stay away from Proctor Hall and telling anyone who'd listen that his daughter's murderer was Noah Proctor."

Julien appeared captivated by the story and asked a lot of questions, most of which the man couldn't answer. He ended his story by saying this was one more unsolved mystery surrounding Proctor Hall.

CHAPTER SIX

The next morning before his first class, Julien went to his office early and searched the web. He wondered what else he could find about the girl's disappearance.

The man had covered almost everything, but Julien found a little more. First, in cases like this, many perpetrators ended up being family members. The cops interviewed Marguey's father but filed no charges, so Landry figured they believed him.

The other interesting item was that Noah would have been forty-nine when the girl disappeared, and the authorities didn't even try to speak with him. Not that it would have mattered, according to tales about the man of no words or emotions.

Once again Noah Proctor and his childhood home became part of a criminal investigation, although there was no proof either played a part in Marguey's disappearance. Once again there were no clues. Julien imagined how this case frustrated the authorities. They must have thought Noah was involved, but without evidence there was nothing they could do.

BILL THOMPSON

In 2018, a reporter visited Proctor Hall to write a "twenty years later" article. He found an abandoned house, tromped around the tall grass and weeds, and walked around the first floor. The doors were hanging off their hinges, windows were broken, and it seemed no one had lived there for some time. Finding the rooms furnished and the beds made, he grew uneasy. It was as if the residents had stepped out for a moment and would be right back. He called the sheriff to report the abandoned house.

People in the area spoke of noises at night and eerie lights moving from window to window on the second floor. Some claimed to have seen the ghosts of Hiram, Susan and May Ellen Proctor roaming the house, looking for their heads. The reporter experienced none of that, but he also admitted he would never set foot in that creepy house again.

As years passed, people forgot about Marguey Slattery. No investigator opened her thin case folder because nothing new ever surfaced.

The story piqued his interest. It had been some time since Julien saw Proctor Hall, and he wondered how the place looked these days. Soon after the semester ended, he drove to Lafourche Parish. Miles of sugarcane fields lined Highway 308, and a few miles south of Thibodaux he passed a stretch of unkempt grass, briars and weeds. A rotting post supported a mailbox that was just one strong breeze away from toppling. On its side in faded black letters was the word "Proctor." Things had deteriorated since his last visit.

He turned down a rutted one-lane road, and the grass that brushed against his car was as high as cornstalks. A few yards down the lane, a recently installed gate with solid iron posts blocked the road. A sign on the gate read, NO TRESPASSING. PRIVATE PROPERTY. FOR INFORMATION CALL (504) 555-2738.

THE PROCTOR HALL HORROR

That was a surprise, and he called the number. A woman with a friendly Southern accent answered, "Louisiana Society for the Paranormal. This is Cate. How may I help you?"

Another surprise. A paranormal society owned the property? He stammered, "Uh, my name's Julien Girard. Dr. Julien Girard from Tulane. I'm...uh, I'm at a place called Proctor Hall. It's in Lafourche Parish..."

"I'm familiar with Proctor Hall, Dr. Girard. You say you're there? Did you get this number from our sign?"

"Yes. I came hoping to see the old house."

"That's not possible at the moment, but let me get some information from you and find out what we can do." She asked for his number and why the house interested him.

"I teach a class on Louisiana culture. Plantation homes, unexplained mysteries, ghost stories — that sort of thing." He mentioned those topics specifically in hopes he'd pique her interest. After all, she worked for a paranormal society. "By the way, where are you all located?"

Cate replied, "We're in New Orleans, in the French Quarter. Let me talk with our director and get back in touch with you. I'll call tomorrow at the latest."

"May I ask who your director is?" He smiled when she told him Henri Duchamp was president of the society.

"Tell Henri that Julien Girard sends his regards."

"You know Mr. Duchamp?"

"I've met him, although I didn't realize he headed the paranormal society. I've used his name in vain a hundred times in my classes. There's no one more knowledgeable about supernatural occurrences in Louisiana."

Cate laughed and agreed, adding, "I've only been here a few months, and I haven't learned who his colleagues are yet. If you have a moment, let me find out if he's available."

Henri picked up, greeted Julien warmly, and asked what he was doing out in the boondocks. The professor told him of his interest in the stories surrounding the old plantation.

"I've been here before, but not recently. I understand why a paranormal society would be interested in Proctor Hall. Tell me how it came about. Do you own the plantation?"

Duchamp explained that a friend and benefactor of the society bought distressed properties at tax and foreclosure auctions. Proctor Hall was his latest, and Henri was managing the property as he prepared to investigate the legends.

Julien had nothing to lose by asking to look around, since he'd made the trip.

Henri turned him down. "I'm afraid I can't allow anyone on the property unsupervised. It's in disrepair, and potential liability is an issue. I know it's a wasted trip for you, but I plan to be up there myself on Wednesday. If you're free, you're welcome to join us." Julien jumped at the chance, and after he hung up, he wondered who Henri was bringing with him.

On Wednesday morning the gate stood open. The tall grass and weeds along the lane obscured his view of the house until he emerged onto a recently mowed yard and saw it fifty yards away. He parked next to a Jeep Grand Cherokee and a Channel Nine TV van, got out and walked the perimeter to get a look at the old place.

THE PROCTOR HALL HORROR

Proctor Hall had never been a showplace like many antebellum mansions in the Deep South. It was a long, low-slung two-story house with covered porches on the back and bayou sides and was built for function, not charm. The paint had peeled, plywood covered some windows, and part of the back porch had rotted away.

The door stood open; he stepped inside and called Henri's name. Soon a familiar face appeared around the corner. Although they hadn't met, Julien recognized Landry Drake, the well-known supernatural investigator for a New Orleans TV station. His being on-site meant there was something significant going on at Proctor Hall, and Julien felt a tinge of excitement. Cameras and equipment were everywhere, and people were tromping around upstairs. That meant a film crew was here.

Landry knew Julien by reputation as a well-respected authority and the author of several textbooks on Louisiana culture. "Dr. Girard?" he said, offering his hand. "I'm Landry Drake. Henri's upstairs; come on in."

"Please call me Julien. Of course I know who you are. It's nice to meet you. I was excited when Henri agreed to let me come, but after seeing you here, I'm more interested than ever! What are you guys up to?"

"Is my name being used in vain?" Henri Duchamp's voice boomed as he walked downstairs. Julien presumed this was the very staircase where Noah Proctor had sat covered in blood after supposedly murdering his family.

After exchanging pleasantries for a moment, Henri suggested they go out to the front porch — the one overlooking Bayou Lafourche — and talk. The old oaks swayed in a light breeze as they sat on the steps. Julien commented on how beautiful the scene was along the tree-lined bayou at the far end of the yard.

"What's your interest in Proctor Hall?" Henri asked.

Julien explained for several years he'd used the old house and its macabre history as part of his course on Louisiana culture. He'd seen it a few times, but not lately. He added, "Since Landry's here, I presume the house is haunted."

"'Haunted' isn't a word I use often," Henri said. "It tends to conjure up thoughts of spectral visitors, unexplained lights, sounds and the like. Something very unusual is happening here, but it's too early to assume anything."

"I appreciate you allowing me to come."

"That permission comes with a caveat," Henri said. "If you choose to stay and observe, everything that happens is confidential. You're free to talk about Proctor Hall so long as what you say comes from outside sources. Unless I approve it, you are prohibited from discussing anything — anything at all — that you see, hear or experience on this property. Do you agree to those conditions?"

"Yes," Julien said. "Yes, of course I do. I'm just pleased to be here today and to get the chance to watch you all at work."

Henri smiled. "Before we start, allow me to give you some history about what I believe to be Louisiana's most haunted plantation."

CHAPTER SEVEN

Landry said, "When you called, you spoke to Henri's assistant, Cate Adams. She's my girlfriend, and her father is a doctor who invests in distressed properties."

"So he owns Proctor Hall?"

"Yes. He recently bought the plantation at a tax auction — the house, a thousand acres, and thirty-five outbuildings, including the ruins of a hundred-year-old sugar mill. The previous owner was Hiram Proctor, who died here in the 1963 massacre. Hiram's caretaker, Ben Trimble, stayed on after the killings — Noah was the only family left, and with him in an institution, no one challenged Ben's living here. Ben paid the property taxes up through 2014. At some point afterwards, it seems they just walked away."

Julien asked, "The caretaker and his wife took care of Noah after his release. When they left, what happened to him?"

Landry said, "That's something I'd like to know. The Trimbles were reclusive — they didn't have any friends or close neighbors. On their rare trips into town, they did their business and got out. As far as Noah, nobody ever saw him after he came home in 1989. The locals concocted stories about Noah being locked up here in what they already called a haunted house. When Marguey Slattery disappeared nine years after Noah's return, everyone assumed he was up to his old tricks.

"As Henri said, they abandoned the house sometime after 2014. In 2018, a reporter doing a follow-up on Marguey's disappearance came here. He called the sheriff's office and reported open doors with nobody around. Deputies gave the house a quick search and found furniture, personal effects, silverware and dishes, and even pans on the stove containing dried meat. It looked like they just walked away."

Landry said people jumped on that story. They used words like "vanished" and "mysterious" and "bizarre" even though their departure might have been as simple as deciding to move away. People chose to believe Noah had struck again. He chopped up Ben and Agnes and cooked them on the stove before he left. That story stuck, even though investigators proved the meat was chicken.

The sheriff reported brown stains on the sitting room rug — the room where Noah had propped up the bodies. The stains resembled blood, but the sheriff figured they happened during the massacre. Without taking samples, he secured the house as best he could and left.

Julien said, "So that reporter was the first to report the house abandoned?"

"It seems so. Everyone believed Proctor Hall was haunted, and people said Noah hid out somewhere in the swamps, awaiting his next victim. The tales have elements of a classic ghost story, but it kept most people away and the house from being looted."

THE PROCTOR HALL HORROR

Henri said they were starting a walkthrough and invited Julien to come along. Julien seemed enthralled by the place and asked to take pictures. Henri said no.

"There are more ghost stories about Proctor Hall than any others I know," Henri said as they went from room to room. The 1963 massacre gave the house a reputation for supernatural occurrences. There were rumors of hidden rooms and passages, an ancient graveyard where Noah Proctor slept at night, chain-rattling spirits that roamed the upstairs bedrooms, and drops of blood that mysteriously appeared on the mantel each year on the anniversary of the massacre.

"As happens so often, some of the tales were based on fact," Henri told them, "but they became distorted in each retelling. Here's one that seems to be true." He paused outside a door in the upstairs hallway.

"Looks normal to me," Landry said as Henri opened the door to reveal a five-foot-square room with metal bars on all four sides and the top and bottom. It looked like a cage at the zoo. Henri opened the barred door and said, "Makes you wonder why the Proctors needed this room."

"What's it for?"

"The story goes that Noah was insane. He was locked here twenty-four hours a day to protect the family. One day he managed to escape, and look how things turned out."

Julien asked, "Could that legend be true?"

Henri shrugged. "There's no way to know. That secret and many others died with the family, I suppose. Noah was a mute, as we know, so he never explained things either."

BILL THOMPSON

Fascinating, Julien thought as they walked on. *So many secrets in one house, and nobody has a clue what really happened at Proctor Hall.*

CHAPTER EIGHT

The semester was drawing to a close. Several of his students would graduate, and as always, Julien would miss some more than others. With just six weeks remaining, he announced one morning how the last assignment for Appreciation of Louisiana Culture would work.

He drew names from a hat, dividing his sixteen students into four teams. On Friday, each team would submit its proposal for a project that embraced and promoted appreciation of Louisiana's culture. Once he approved the projects, the teams would go to work. This assignment would make up forty percent of the class grade, and only the winning team would receive an A. The others would get a B or below, based on several factors.

The winning team would best embody the spirit and history of Louisiana. The amount and depth of research, on-site work if necessary, creativity and imagination would be factors in the ultimate grade. He encouraged out-of-the-box thinking and said nothing lawful and moral was off the table.

BILL THOMPSON

"You'll have two weeks to complete your project," Julien explained. "They're due three weeks before the end of the semester, so you'll have plenty of time to study for finals in your other courses. Just before summer break I'll name the winners and post everyone's grades."

He drew names and wrote the team participants on a whiteboard. He chuckled to himself at the makeup of Team B. A struggling student who needed the grade, a football player on a scholarship, and two type A's — Marisol, the smug know-it-all and Andy Arnaud, the class clown and smartass.

As his students looked at the team makeups, he noticed discomfort on some faces. As far as Julien knew, these people weren't close friends. Except for this class, they were strangers. It would be fascinating to observe the dynamics, and that was one reason he'd rigged the drawing.

Julien Girard had handpicked these four, knowing without a doubt they would choose the project he wanted them to have. The driven, aggressive Marisol would make it happen.

On Friday, the students revealed their projects. Three teams chose ones that were mundane and predictable. Over the years, other teams had chosen the same ones, and they'd long ceased to be interesting to Julien. The long, colorful history of one Garden District mansion. The impact of Hurricane Katrina on New Orleans society and commerce. Sites where the pirate Jean Lafitte plied his trade and sold his booty.

Every boring project would be well-researched, polished and neatly wrapped for presentation at the end of term. Each team hoped for an A in this class where A's weren't easily earned. And none of them would get it.

THE PROCTOR HALL HORROR

His heart jumped when he called on Team B and Marisol stood to announce their project — the mysterious history of Proctor Hall.

Just as I thought! They took the bait!

Julien accepted all four submissions and read a list of caveats. No trespassing — you must have permission before going on private property. No plagiarism — the words in their final reports must be their own or footnoted with attribution. And the majority ruled. Anything the team did required three votes in favor.

He would not see them again for two weeks. Instead of three hours a week in his classroom, they would use the time collaborating, researching and doing what they could to create a winning project.

Julien found it difficult to contain his excitement. It would be hard to wait.

CHAPTER NINE

The four couldn't have been more diverse, which had been Julien Girard's plan. They sat around a table at Starbucks, and Marisol declared herself the logical choice for team leader.

Michael and April didn't care who was in charge, so long as it wasn't them. He was a sophomore on a football scholarship, and a passing grade was all he wanted. It would suit him if the others did the project while he worked out in the gym.

Also a sophomore, April was from Natchez, and she was a history major like Marisol. That choice frustrated her parents, who said the only thing a history degree was good for was teaching, but that was just what April wanted. School was hard for her, and she needed a good grade in Dr. Girard's class. For that reason, she'd do her part to make this project the winner.

"What qualifies you to be leader?" Andy snorted.

BILL THOMPSON

"What qualifies me is that I'm both smart and crafty, and I'm not an obnoxious rich asshole like someone on our team."

"Run the damn thing. Do everything yourself, for all I care. That's what you want anyway. We'll just sit back and watch."

"No, you won't. This is a team project, and we'll do it as a team. I'll assign work to the three of you, tackle the harder tasks myself, and between us we'll turn in the best report and get that A."

Andy wouldn't let it go. "You're saying thanks to your hard work, the team will end up with an A? You think you're hot stuff, but the guys can do the heavy lifting on this one, little lady."

She slapped him so quickly it astonished not only Andy, but everyone else in the coffee shop. "Don't you ever belittle me again, you coonass misogynist," she hissed. She regained her composure, forced a smile to her face, and said, "Where were we?"

After that encounter, a vote wasn't necessary. Marisol was de facto leader, and the consensus was to visit Proctor Hall. She assigned Andy to find the owner and get permission. April and Michael got research jobs — she on the massacre in 1963 and he on Marguey Slattery's disappearance in 1998.

Andy sneered, "How about you? Are you going to sit around eating bonbons while we do your bidding?"

"I'll find out what happened to Noah Proctor."

Andy texted the others at five that afternoon. *All good for our visit to Proctor Hall. I'll pick you up tomorrow*

THE PROCTOR HALL HORROR

morning at eight on Freret Street by the library. Black Ram pickup.

Surprised Andy could have gotten them in that fast, Marisol texted back.

Who gave you permission? Is someone meeting us there?

You do your job. I'll do mine. We're in. See you tomorrow at eight.

Damn. This was how the entire project would be, and she had to get over it. Fighting with Andy wouldn't get them the top grade.

His Dodge pickup was the biggest, baddest, most jacked-up thing she'd ever seen. It had a dealer tag — she knew his dad owned several dealerships, since Andy bragged about it to everyone — and it was downright luxurious inside. She took the front passenger seat, and as they got on the interstate, she turned down the blaring rock music and asked him who gave him permission to go inside Proctor Hall.

"You just can't stand it, can you? Somebody else is more resourceful than the great Marisol. Just settle back and take it easy. If you can, that is. I don't think you're wired to relax, but you should give it a try sometime."

She let it go. She admitted to herself this was one fine ride, and Andy was a far better driver than she expected. *I'll bet he's afraid he'll wreck Daddy's car.* She dismissed the catty thought in the interest of harmony and a common goal.

They pulled up to the gate, and she asked whose phone number was on the sign.

"Some paranormal outfit." He got out of the car and said, "We walk from here."

April said, "A paranormal outfit? What do you mean?"

"I mean the message on their phone said they were some kind of paranormal society."

Marisol said, "Am I the only one who thinks that's weird? We're at an old house where a kid decapitated his mother, father and little sister. Years later, another girl disappeared here. And it belongs to a paranormal organization? I'm not afraid myself, but does anyone think this might be dangerous?"

"Dangerous? It's just an old house, for God's sake. This isn't some horror flick or Stephen King novel. Wait until you see it. It's not a spooky old mansion like what you expect in this part of Louisiana."

April wasn't convinced. "It makes no sense why a paranormal group would own this place."

"Perhaps they don't," Marisol said. "Maybe they're investigating the stories about Proctor Hall, and when they're done, they'll take down the sign. Speaking of that, the gate's got a lock and chain on it. How do we get in?"

Andy said, "We climb over the gate."

"Isn't that trespassing?" April asked, and Marisol insisted Andy explain or they were leaving.

"I drove up yesterday after I left you guys," he said. "I parked here and called the number. Then I climbed over and walked to the house. It's less than a quarter of a mile — you just can't see it because of the tall grass."

"They told you to climb over the gate?"

THE PROCTOR HALL HORROR

"Nobody said I couldn't. Okay, so I got an answering machine. Some paranormal society, like I said. I left a message that we would be here this morning to visit the house unless they told me no. They never called, so it must be okay with them."

Marisol snapped, "Yesterday was Saturday, dammit. You knew when you left the message they might close on weekends. They haven't even listened to it yet."

He raised his eyebrows, turned to April and Michael, and said, "It takes three votes to approve a decision. There hasn't been anybody at Proctor Hall in years, as far as I could tell. Who cares if we just look around?"

"How about the person who put up the No Trespassing sign?" Marisol said. "Dr. Girard told us we couldn't do anything illegal, so instead of following the rules, you left a message when you figured they wouldn't get it. I vote no. This is wrong."

Andy wanted to run things, and now was the time to take charge. They had voted her team leader over his objection, so it was time for persuasion. It worked with the girls he dated, and it could work now.

"Guys, we're here. The house is just down that lane, nobody's around, and there's nothing to stop us from checking it out. I'm not talking about spending the night inside. I'm saying we should just go look around."

It made sense to Michael, and April said, "Since you put it that way, why not?"

Marisol shrugged. "All right, but let's speed it up. The sooner we're out of here, the better." Michael, the football player, vaulted the gate with ease, followed by Andy, who offered a hand to help April. When he did the same to

Marisol, she said, "I don't need any help from you, thanks," and climbed the gate. Her jeans snagged on a piece of wire at the top, and she ripped a hole in her pants leg as she swung over. Andy smirked as she brushed herself off and followed the others down the narrow lane.

Once in sight of the old farmhouse, Andy said, "It's all locked up. The other side has a porch like this one that looks out over Bayou Lafourche."

Marisol walked around taking pictures with her phone. "It is in awful shape," she commented, and Andy said the inside was just as bad.

She spun around. "You went inside? Dammit, you're going to get us all in trouble, and you don't seem to give a rat's ass about it. Let's go. We're done here."

"Since we came all this way, we might as well finish looking around," he said, but she stalked off across the yard.

Marisol headed for the pickup, but before she got to the narrow lane, a woman walked into the yard. She was a little older than they were, and she didn't look happy. After talking to Marisol for a moment, they walked to the house together.

"This is Cate Adams," Marisol said as the others joined them. "She's with the Louisiana Society for the Paranormal. I tried to explain..."

Cate interrupted. "You say this is some kind of college field trip. There's a sign on the gate. Which one of you guys called the office?"

"That would be me," Andy said, turning on his best bullshit smile.

THE PROCTOR HALL HORROR

"And by leaving a message, what right did that give you to trespass on private property? I'm calling the sheriff."

April started crying, and Marisol said, "Miss Adams, I'll apologize for the group. This isn't a field trip. We're a team working on a class project. We chose Proctor Hall because of its interesting history."

"What class? Where do you go to school?"

"Tulane. It's Dr. Girard's class called Appreciation of Louisiana Culture."

"Julien Girard?"

"Yes." She knew him, and Marisol hoped that meant they weren't going to jail.

Cate pulled out her phone, told them to stay put, and walked away. Moments later she returned.

"Your story checks out, but Julien says he instructed you to get permission before entering private property."

Andy grinned. "My bad. I thought leaving a message was sufficient."

"Bullshit, buddy. You figured you'd be in and out of Proctor Hall before anybody realized you came. By chance I stopped by the office early this morning, and after I heard your message, I drove straight here."

April apologized, saying she wished they hadn't done it, and at last Cate said, "Since you're here, let's go sit on the porch. I want to hear about this project of yours."

Andy started talking, and Cate raised her hand to shush him. "Not you." She looked at April. "I want to hear it from you."

Unaccustomed to playing second fiddle and dying to interrupt and tell the story, Marisol fumed. April was a decent person, but she wasn't eloquent, and it irritated Marisol no end that she wasn't the one doing the talking.

April began with an apology and explained why they came. By the time she finished, Cate found herself liking them. April and Michael were followers, but even the narcissistic Andy was tolerable. Only Marisol rubbed her the wrong way somehow — she seemed to have this need to be in charge that annoyed Cate. She was a driven individual. *Ruthless* was another word that came to mind.

Maybe she irritates me because we're a lot alike, Cate thought. *Let it go.*

She said, "Dr. Girard confirmed your story, although you broke the rules by not asking permission." She shot a stern glance at Andy. "*You* know what I mean. I work for a man named Henri Duchamp, who's a friend of your professor's. He founded the Louisiana Society for the Paranormal, and he's just begun a project here. You know the history of Proctor Hall, and you came here intending to poke around and see what might happen. You might even have gone inside on your own, and that could have been disastrous for you.

"The word *haunted* doesn't do Proctor Hall justice. The awful murders within these walls — what people call the Massacre at Proctor Hall — are only part of what happened here. Over the years this property has had more documented paranormal activity than any other plantation home in Louisiana. I'll take you inside. We'll stay together and you'll do everything I say. If anyone disobeys, all of you will leave."

THE PROCTOR HALL HORROR

She unlocked the door and stepped through. When they joined her in the hallway, they saw tripods and stage lights stacked in an adjoining room.

"Is somebody filming a movie here?" Andy asked, and Cate said the society was filming a documentary about Proctor Hall.

"Look at the name stenciled on the stuff," Michael said, pointing. "WCCY-TV. That's the station Landry Drake works for."

That opened a can of worms Cate had hoped to keep closed.

CHAPTER TEN

"He's right. That is Landry Drake's station," Marisol said. "The ghost hunter. How exciting that he's doing a show right in this very house!"

Cate hedged. "Not everything WCCY-TV does is his work."

Marisol snorted. "You expect us to believe he's not involved in a house you say is way more than just 'haunted'? You have my attention. Tell us the truth. What's going on here?"

Cate wouldn't have let them in if she realized Landry's crew had left behind the camera equipment after their last shoot. Angry at herself, she wondered how little she could get away with saying and still placate them.

"Landry Drake and Henri Duchamp, the president of our society, have worked together for years. I work for Henri, and the society is managing Proctor Hall for its owner. I heard a Channel Nine film crew did a shoot here — background video that may be aired someday. It appears they left some equipment behind."

Andy said, "So you're saying Landry himself wasn't here? Only a crew from his station came?"

Be careful, Cate. "I wasn't here when they were, so I can't say who came."

"Who owns the property now?" Marisol asked. "If Noel's the only Proctor left, is he the owner?"

"The owner is a corporation." Another answer that wasn't an answer.

She pushed Cate for more. "You work for the paranormal society, so you know who owns the house, but you're not telling. Why is that?"

Cate had had enough. "Because it's none of your business. You need to learn when to ease off a little, my friend. Before you piss me off, do you all want to see more of the house, or are we done here?"

April said, "Yes, please. Let's look at the house. Marisol, knock it off. This isn't an interrogation."

Cate exhaled and hoped Landry would have handled things as she did. She decided there wasn't much else she could have done as she showed them the stair riser where Noah Proctor had sat covered in blood the day his family died.

If Marisol had further questions, she kept them to herself. April asked how much time Cate had spent in the house and learned this was only her third visit and she hadn't experienced anything unusual.

She took them down the hall and into a sitting room. The moment they entered, April uttered a deep sigh and said, "This room is a place of tragedy and sorrow — and evil. The house is filled with evil."

THE PROCTOR HALL HORROR

Cate said, "Why do you say that? Do you have psychic powers?"

Her eyes closed, April nodded. "They didn't die in this room, though. The evil one brought them from…another place. Somewhere else. Their heads…"

A thunderous crash came from outside the room, startling them. "What the hell was that?" Andy shouted.

"Them. It was them," April said. "I disturbed them."

They left the room and found a large antique hall tree toppled over and blocking the hall. The piece was solid oak and very heavy, and it had tipped forward so its legs touched one wall while the top rested against the opposite one.

Michael tried to upend it, but couldn't until Andy gave him a hand. "This thing must weigh three hundred pounds," he said. "There's no way it fell over by itself."

"It didn't," April said. "They knocked it over."

"They who?" Andy said. "Stop talking like you're a fortune-teller or something. Nobody else is here. Who the hell are 'they'?"

Without responding, April returned to the sitting room. Cate followed and said, "Are you sensing things, or are you also seeing them?"

"They told me what happened here." She pointed to the mantel. "That's where their heads were."

Cate stepped out of the box and asked a bold question. "Did Noah Proctor kill his family?"

April walked to the mantel and touched it lightly. "So much tragedy." Then she turned and joined the others in the hall.

Cate let it go. It might not have been smart to ask the question. Although April had never been to Proctor Hall, Cate believed what she said. She and Landry had experienced the supernatural countless times, and she had a healthy respect for things that defied explanation.

Upstairs was a long hallway wider than the one below, with two bedrooms on each side. Faded wall coverings, tattered curtains and dust-covered furniture gave the rooms a depressing air. Cate sensed abandonment as she glanced in each room. People had slept in these beds once, but one day long ago someone had murdered them one by one.

Maybe this was Noah's room. Why did he leave, and where did he go? Is he still alive?

Cate realized April wasn't with the group and found her at the far end of the hallway in the shadows.

"What are you feeling now?"

She pointed to a bedroom door. "I can't go in there."

"Why not?"

"It will smother me. I'll die if I walk through that door." She trembled.

"We should go," Cate said, taking her hand. But April pulled away.

"I need to face this. So much is wrong about this house — so much that we have to uncover. Only then can they rest. Only then." She walked to the door and looked inside.

THE PROCTOR HALL HORROR

She uttered a ghastly shriek — something feral and terrifying — and collapsed.

Cate knelt beside her. "What do you see?"

"In the bed. They're…it's all about the bed."

Andy walked into the gloomy room. "Smells like something rotten in here," he said with a grimace, "but the bed's empty. The covers are all messed up like somebody forgot to make it, but nobody's here. You thought you saw something…"

"Get me out of here!" April screamed, squeezing Cate's hand. "It's smothering me! I can't breathe."

As easily as lifting a book, Michael swept April up into his arms and carried her downstairs and out onto the porch. She gasped for each breath, but the moment they were outdoors, she breathed normally again, as though an oppressive weight on her chest was gone.

The group walked back to the car, and Cate asked April to describe what had happened.

"When I reached the bedroom door, I felt something drawing me in. Sucking, pulling, like a vacuum cleaner. The closer I came to going inside, the more I felt it *wanting* me."

"What did you see in the bed?"

"I…I can't describe it. Something horrible. Not a person — a *thing*. I don't want to think about it. I've never been so scared in my life."

Cate moved her Jeep to allow them to leave, and returned to Proctor Hall. As she reached for the door to close and lock it, something inside the house caught her eye.

BILL THOMPSON

Something moved on the stairway. A dark shape — a person, maybe. More like a shadow, but what light filtered into the house wasn't enough to create shadows.

Now she saw it. A boy.

Sitting on the staircase. Looking at her.

Noah Proctor.

CHAPTER ELEVEN

In Andy's opinion, Marisol was "holding court." She'd convened the team to talk about yesterday's trip to Proctor Hall, and her first order of business was to lash out at him.

"We might have been arrested! You lied to us and let us go when you had no permission at all. That's the last time…"

"Lighten up, okay? Everything worked out fine. We got inside until April made a scene and screwed things up. We even know the great Landry Drake's involved. That woman was lying when she told us he wasn't."

April was hurt. "I can see things sometimes, things other people can't. I'm not proud of my power. I couldn't help what happened. There are bad things in that house."

Andy shook his head. "It's a house like a million others. When somebody abandons an old house in south Louisiana, people make up stories about hauntings. They claim spooks ran off the family, or killed them and buried them in the backyard or something. This one's cut and dried. A crazy kid murdered his entire family. That's it."

Marisol disagreed. She accepted that paranormal things could happen, and she asked April how long she'd had psychic abilities.

"A few years. Usually my experiences aren't scary like yesterday. Sometimes I use a Ouija board."

"Whoa!" Andy cried. "This is crazy. Not only can you see things that aren't there, you also summon up ghosts and stuff? You're making all this up."

April said, "I don't want to be on the team anymore. I don't like this project, and I'm not safe at Proctor Hall. You all don't seem to understand. Maybe you don't care."

Michael asked why she considered it unsafe. It had been empty for years. What harm was there in looking around in the daytime? She didn't have to go upstairs if it made her uncomfortable.

He added, "Before yesterday I didn't care about this project either, to be honest. I was just going to let Marisol run the show and coast along to an A. But if Landry Drake's interested in this place, we need to see what's up."

Negative thoughts rushed through Marisol's mind. *What would Dr. Girard do if a team member resigned? Would it cost them a shot at the highest grade for the project?* She couldn't risk it; she had to keep the team together.

"Michael's right, April. We respect that you have psychic powers. If we want the top grade, we must go back to Proctor Hall. I don't know how we'll get in, but I promise you we'll stick together. We'll protect you. Please don't jump ship on us. We all need an A in this course, and I'll make sure we get it."

Uneasy but unwilling to rock the boat, April agreed to stay, which relieved Marisol. Once again she promised to keep

THE PROCTOR HALL HORROR

her safe. That flippant, throwaway comment would haunt Marisol later.

CHAPTER TWELVE

On the way back to New Orleans, Cate called Landry to find out where he was.

He laughed. "It's Sunday morning, so I'm either at the apartment or getting coffee in the Quarter. The question is where are you? You left three hours ago to run by your office for a minute. You must have lost track of time."

She said, "I had to go to Proctor Hall. Something crazy happened. I'll tell you when I get home."

"I heard you were there, to tell the truth. Julien Girard just called me to apologize for his students' behavior. What happened?"

"I'm too rattled to talk and drive. Let's have brunch at Muriel's. I'll meet you at one."

She walked from the garage on Governor Nicholls Street to Jackson Square. As she passed the artists who displayed their work on the fence around the square, she heard lively music through the front doors of the restaurant a half block away. Muriel's occupied an eighteenth-century building and had what Landry considered the Quarter's best Sunday jazz brunch.

Their favorite maître d' Claude greeted her by name and escorted her to Landry's table on the balcony. The day was perfect for outdoor dining, and the view was spectacular. There stood St. Louis Cathedral just steps away, and Jackson Square was teeming with people. A cold bottle of Chardonnay sat beside the table, but when she noticed Landry's Bloody Mary, she ordered one too.

"So you ran off some kids."

"That's what I intended to do, but things changed. They were trespassing; one of them is a smart-ass kid who left me a voicemail saying they wanted to visit the house. If we didn't respond, he'd take it as a yes."

"That's brazen," Landry commented as her drink arrived, and they clinked glasses in a toast to living in the same town after long-distance dating all these years.

"Like I said, he's full of himself. Anyway, I decided since they came all that way, I'd let them go inside. Oh, they noticed your camera equipment. That got everyone excited."

"Yeah, since we're going back sometime this week, I told the crew to leave it."

"One of them is a shy girl who's a clairvoyant. Something in an upstairs bedroom spooked the hell out of her."

Landry said, "We'll look into that bedroom. I'll ask Henri if he knows anything. Wonder if it might be Noah Proctor's."

THE PROCTOR HALL HORROR

She shrugged off a shiver. "I saw Noah. Or an apparition. Sitting on the stairs, looking at me. It scared me, and I think I dropped the keys. I can't find them now."

"I'll get them when Henri and I go back up. No big deal; we've had no trouble since we posted the no-trespassing sign."

His phone rang. He looked at the screen, smiled and answered. "Speak of the devil. Cate had an interesting experience at Proctor Hall this morning. I'll tell you about it when we get together." He paused a moment, raised his eyebrows, and looked at Cate, who nodded. "We're at Muriel's. Come join us for lunch."

Henri arrived, hugged Cate, greeted Landry, and took a seat. He ordered a glass of Châteauneuf-du-Pape and listened as Cate described her escapade at Proctor Hall earlier that day.

The psychic girl interested him, but his questions were about Noah Proctor. Was it him or an apparition? He wanted to know how Noah looked — his appearance, clothing and the like.

"I only saw him for a moment," she said. "He looked...well, normal, I guess you'd say. His eyes scared me, like he was burning a hole into mine."

"How old did he appear to be? If he's alive, he'd be around fifty now."

She shook her head. "The person I saw was a teenager. Loose-fitting shirt and pants. Sad. In just those few seconds I sensed a deep sadness."

"You saw his spirit, but I wonder if Noah's still alive."

She worked for Henri, and she apologized for allowing the students inside. No harm done this time, he said, adding that it couldn't happen again. Something in the house worried him.

"Proctor Hall is unique. It's unlike any I've come across in my thirty-plus years investigating the paranormal. There are dark forces at work. I sensed them the other day, and they're malevolent beyond imagination. The house has secrets that someone intends to keep hidden away. People assume the Noah Proctor story is all there is to know about the place, but I'm certain other things — evil things — lurk in there. They might predate the massacre, but perhaps they arose because of it."

Cate sat speechless and surprised at her lack of judgment. She'd opened the house to four young strangers and gone inside herself. According to Henri, the place ranked high among supernatural venues. She felt nothing unusual, but April did. And then there was Noah sitting there on his stair, watching her.

"I can't say it was Noah," she said. "I've never even seen a picture. Perhaps it was someone else, such as another trespasser. What's your take, Henri?"

"The person on the stairs was Noah."

"How can you be certain?"

Henri said, "Because the other day when Landry, Julien and I were at the house, I saw him too. In the same place, wearing the same clothing. The person you saw was Noah in 1963 at the time of the massacre."

CHAPTER THIRTEEN

Andy had no predetermined plan for his nocturnal visit to Proctor Hall. He wanted to show Marisol and the others that he should be team leader. If there was anything to the spooky stories about Proctor Hall, he'd find out. If not, he'd debunk the mystery. Either way, he'd save the day and take the credit. He'd be done by daybreak and report his findings at the team meeting tomorrow morning.

Crickets and cicadas buzzed in the live oak trees as he scaled the gate and walked down the lane. A half-moon hung in the cloudless sky, providing plenty of light for his trek to the house.

He paused as it came into view. *Is that a light moving across the upstairs windows?* When he looked again, he saw nothing, and he blamed it on the moon's reflection.

He'd planned to break a window, but he found a key ring the lady must have dropped on the porch. As he stepped inside, he heard a deep, resonant sound — a bassoon-like hum as if a motor was purring along somewhere deep in the house.

He knew the staircase lay just a few steps away, but the shadows hid the steps where Noah once sat. He directed the flashlight on his phone around the entryway, and as his beam passed the stairs, he noticed something there. When he looked again, the stairs were empty.

Might as well start where the shit hit the fan. He used the light to navigate the inky blackness of the hall past the hall tree that toppled the last time, and walked into the sitting room.

The first thing he noticed was the fetid, offensive air, evoking memories of a smell he couldn't quite recall. He played the light around the room and found everything just as before. He ran his fingers over the wood mantel where the Proctor heads had been. Something behind him rustled softly. He jerked around, but the narrow beam of light revealed nothing.

There in the shadows, moving back and forth in the doorway! Is that something?

On edge and wary now, Andy swept the beam too fast once again. He passed over something — a figure, but perhaps just a lamp standing in a corner. He cried out as a shadow moved across his beam of light, but he decided it had been the moonlight. Now something was behind him, over there by the mantel. His heart beating hard, he turned.

Nothing. Nothing except a heavy sigh, long and despondent, from the hallway behind him. Or perhaps from that corner. He jerked the light here and there and felt something strange in his hand. The light revealed he'd cut himself, and there was a lot of blood. Strange that he felt no pain.

There came another sound and another hazy movement in the dark. The room filled with things he sensed but couldn't see. Something touched his arm while another brushed the

THE PROCTOR HALL HORROR

nape of his neck. And that smell, a hundred times stronger now — repulsive and overpowering.

He remembered the stench from an autumn day long ago. Hunting deer with his father. They'd come upon a bloated cow the coyotes had killed. The rotten, nasty stench of a corpse.

Andy ran toward the door as he struggled to breathe. He sucked in huge gasps, his head began to spin, and he hyperventilated. When he lost consciousness, he fell onto that same couch where the Proctor bodies once sat in a row.

He opened his eyes and looked at his watch. It was a little past one; he hadn't been out for long. He recalled the repugnant smell and fainting, but the odor and the blood on his hand were gone.

Am I dreaming?

Searching for his phone, his fingers ran across soft fabric. He recalled fainting on the couch, but this was someplace else. He found the phone next to him, switched on the flashlight, and looked around. Filmy gauze was everywhere, as if he lay in a cage with walls of wispy cloth, lying on something plush and comfortable.

Am I still in Proctor Hall?

He touched the material with his left hand and pulled it aside. Now he understood where and what, but not how.

I'm in a bedroom — in a four-poster bed with the netting people used in the old days to keep out mosquitoes. But how did I get here? I passed out in the parlor.

Oh, hell! I'm in her room — the Proctor girl — the room that scared April so much the other day. I have to get out of here!

BILL THOMPSON

Andy pushed up with both arms to extricate himself from the feathery mattress. The awful smell returned, and he realized something lay next to him in the plush bed. He turned the flashlight on.

A body lay inches away from him. A girl, by the looks of the clothes, and so close he could touch it, but he had no desire to do that.

Like that cow he and his dad found, she'd been dead a long time.

He thought his head would explode. He struggled to breathe as the room spun crazily. Then something snapped, and he began to laugh. A tinny cackle at first, then louder and louder until his maniacal howls resounded inside the netting and throughout the old house. *Hahahahaha,* he shrieked over and over until his throat turned raspy and dry.

As he stood, he saw a lot more blood, this time on the pillow where she would rest her head.

If she'd had one.

CHAPTER FOURTEEN

Andy didn't show up for the Wednesday team meeting, and no one had spoken with him. Marisol texted and waited a few minutes before starting.

The meeting ended with no word from Andy, which was unlike him. He wasn't Mirasol's favorite person — far from it — but she was concerned. She called this time, got voicemail, and asked him to check in.

At the same time Marisol's team met, Landry drove to Thibodaux. Henri and Channel Nine's head photographer Phil Vandegriff rode with him. Today they intended to shoot video in every room of Proctor Hall.

When they pulled up to the gate, they found a black pickup blocking the road. Landry honked a few times, but no one came. He parked behind it, unlocked the gate, and they walked to the house.

Landry found Cate's key ring with the house key inserted in the lock. They stepped inside, and Landry put a finger to his lips. Someone was upstairs — maybe more than one.

They heard indistinct words, laughter and dry coughs. As they ascended the stairway, the sounds became clearer.

They reached the top of the stairs and walked into the hall. "Who's there?" Henri shouted, and the noise stopped. Four bedroom doors stood open.

"Who's here?" Landry said.

"Here. We're in here." More hoarse coughs followed.

They ran to a bedroom at the end of the hall and found a young man sitting on the floor. Next to him was an old Victorian four-poster bed shrouded in opaque netting. Landry figured the boy was in his early twenties; from the way his eyes bulged and he laughed, Landry thought he was in shock.

"Who are you?" Henri asked.

The boy's reply came as a throaty growl, "That's not as important as finding out who's in there." He pointed to the bed and flashed a crazed smile.

Landry jerked the gauze back and found a plush down mattress and oversized pillows. "There's nobody in here."

Andy stopped laughing. "That's odd. A girl with no head lay there earlier this morning."

"Who are you?"

He furrowed his brow, seemingly stumped by the innocuous question. He thought for a moment and said, "I don't know. I was Andy Arnaud when I came, but things seem completely different now. Could I be someone else?"

On a hunch, Landry called Julien Girard, who confirmed Andy was a member of the team investigating Proctor Hall.

THE PROCTOR HALL HORROR

When Landry described the scene, Julien asked to speak with the boy.

"He's babbling nonsense and laughing uncontrollably. There's no use trying to talk to him. Tell me this — what color is Andy's hair?"

Wondering why he asked such a strange question, Julien said Andy had a full head of black hair. "Why do you ask?"

"Because it isn't black anymore. Now it's as white as snow. Something traumatic happened to him — something monumental enough to change him physically as well as mentally. I hope we can find out what."

CHAPTER FIFTEEN

Harry Kanter had a problem, and that problem had a name.

Landry Drake.

"Why me?" he wondered as his boss tossed a file on his desk and said his friend the ghost hunter was in the middle of a new case.

"I keep telling you he's not my friend," Kanter said, but the major shook his head. Nobody else on the state police force knew Landry, so the case was his.

"You know who David Arnaud is, right?"

He recognized the name. Anyone who watched TV knew it, because David Arnaud owned car dealerships all over south Louisiana. You couldn't watch a football game or a sitcom or the news without getting invited to buy a car from Dealin' Dave Arnaud.

"Something weird happened to Arnaud's kid inside an old house near Thibodaux. They found him babbling crazy shit about a dead body, his hair turned white within seconds — stuff that makes no sense."

"What's the crime?"

"Beats me. I can't see where he committed a crime. If the kid broke in, then it could be trespassing. Regardless, we're checking it out. I got a call from the top telling me to send somebody down there ASAP."

"The top? What the hell are you talking about? The governor's office?"

His boss nodded. "Dealin' Dave has some influential friends."

"How does Landry play into this?"

"Your friend the ghost hunter? He's the one who found Dave's son Andy stark raving mad inside Proctor Hall."

Harry didn't call Landry his friend because that word didn't describe their relationship. Landry was a colleague, someone Harry enjoyed working with. His first case involving the paranormal investigator had been at an abandoned insane asylum in Iberia Parish. Landry had called on him several times since then, and each case was more fascinating than the last.

He checked out a sedan and drove with a young patrolman to Thibodaux. Per protocol, they stopped first at the sheriff's office as a courtesy notice. The sheriff didn't understand why they came at first. His deputy had been at the house for hours. Some kid had a problem at Proctor Hall, but there was no crime to investigate. When he heard the request came from the governor's office, he was even more confused.

THE PROCTOR HALL HORROR

"Nothing happened out there. I figure he got high on something," the sheriff said. "Hallucinating, talking about seeing dead bodies, all that stuff. He'll be fine when he comes down. What's the big deal?"

"You got me," Harry admitted. "We'll stop by the house and look around. Send someone along if you wish. Either way, I'll stop by here before we head back to Baton Rouge." The sheriff said he'd notify the deputy on the scene and await Harry's report.

"We meet again," Harry said as he met Landry in the downstairs hallway. Landry brought him up to speed, and they agreed there was nothing to investigate.

"Where's the boy now?"

"His mother picked him up an hour ago. I guess she took him home."

"What do you make of his hair turning white?"

"People claim it can happen. It's called Marie Antoinette syndrome because it's reputed to have happened to her on the night before her execution. If I hadn't seen it myself, I would never have believed it could happen, but there's no doubt about it. His mother went to pieces when she saw him."

Harry asked about the boy's story of a headless girl in the bed, and Landry gave him an abbreviated version of the Massacre at Proctor Hall. "Andy was studying the murders as part of a class at Tulane," he added. "Consider this idea. It's nothing but a theory, because we won't learn the truth unless Andy tells us. I think he hallucinated about Noah's dead sister to such an extent that the scene became real in his mind. He played a role in an event so horrifying that his mind short-circuited."

The sheriff's assessment had been on target, and it jived with Landry's. It looked like the boy got high at a haunted house he'd visited before, and had visions that screwed up his mind. He didn't believe the white hair story. Could be the kid bleached it before he came. Or something else happened. People's hair just didn't turn colors because they had a little fright.

While the young patrolman drove them back to Baton Rouge, Harry called Andy Arnaud's mother as a courtesy. A psychiatrist friend of the family was at the house with Andy. *The family shrink,* Harry mused as he gave the lady his number and asked her to stay in touch. Back at headquarters, he reported to his boss, who called the state house. Crisis averted, everyone accounted for, and the fastest ending to an encounter with Landry Drake in history.

Or so it appeared.

CHAPTER SIXTEEN

Henri's story about finding Andy worried Julien. For years he'd sent students off on end-of-term projects, and until now nothing had gone wrong. This time, because of his selfish personal desires, he'd steered this team into danger — Proctor Hall.

Understanding what might happen, he'd allowed them to go anyway. With full knowledge of the dark things there, he'd still encouraged them to take this project. His motive was to see if the team was clever enough to uncover the secrets inside, but this time his game backfired. Thank God the kid was alive. Unimaginable things might have happened at any moment; the consequences would have been disastrous for Julien.

He called Landry to apologize. "I'm pulling them off right now. It's all my fault; when they suggested Proctor Hall for their semester project, I said yes contingent on their getting permission, which I doubted was possible. They ignored my orders about trespass not once, but twice. From now on I'll choose the projects instead of letting the students do it."

Landry said, "Keep your fingers crossed Andy recovers with no lasting harm done. Don't be too hard on yourself. You did what you should have. I want to ask you about Proctor Hall. Are you familiar with the stories about it being one of the area's most haunted houses?"

"I know more than the average person, I guess. I've done considerable research because the place fascinates me. First the massacre happens, later Marguey Slattery vanishes, and people blame Noah Proctor for both. It's a fascinating place."

Landry asked if Julien had told the team about Andy. He hadn't, but Marisol, the team leader, had called while he was speaking with Landry. "I'm sure she's heard it by now. I'll cancel the project as soon as we're finished talking."

"I have an idea. Let me continue the project in collaboration with just one of your students. Cate told me that April is a clairvoyant who felt things at Proctor Hall. Unless you object, I want to ask if she'd work with me. The others can come along too, but it's April I need. Her psychic powers might uncover the secrets."

"I like the idea. It would change the dynamics of the project I assigned. The chance to work with you gives them a huge edge over the other teams. I'll work that part out. I'll call the kids in and see what happens."

He emailed Marisol, Michael and April, asking them to come by his office that afternoon. Then he leaned back in his chair, laced his fingers behind his head, and wondered if this was the right thing to do.

How did Landry put it? — *Her psychic powers might uncover Proctor Hall's secrets.*

This was the first he'd learned about April being a psychic, and it added an interesting layer to the situation. What might they discover if she teamed up with the famous investigative reporter and ghost hunter? How interesting that might be!

Here came that old feeling again, that excitement of knowing someone was seeking answers at Proctor Hall. How close might they come to learning the truth?

I hope April agrees to work with him. I'd be fascinated to watch their progress.

When they met, Julien told the kids what had happened to their teammate Andy. There were rumors, but the truth astounded Marisol and Michael. April seemed disconnected as she sat with her hands folded in her lap.

When he said Landry Drake wanted them to team up with him, Marisol gave a whoop of joy. "The chance to work with a TV personality! Wow. You don't have to ask me twice!" Michael was in too. He said it sounded like fun to watch a ghost hunter at work.

"Do we still get the A, even though we're working with a pro?" Marisol was always the opportunist. Even with a chance like this, she still wanted that top grade.

"If Landry says your effort deserves it, you will."

April was the critical one, but she said nothing. She stared at the wall as if lost in thought until Marisol said, "You're in, right, April? What an opportunity!"

No response.

Julien said, "Do you need more time to mull it over? How about until tomorrow?"

"I don't need more time. I told the others earlier I didn't like this project. Something awful is in that house, and you know that too, Dr. Girard. Consider what it did to Andy, and what happened to me when we were there. Something horrific inhabits Proctor Hall. Upstairs in a bedroom. An entity so evil it wants to kill us all."

Julien shot Marisol a look, and she rolled her eyes dramatically. He was glad April was staring into her lap and hadn't noticed.

Julien asked April if meeting Landry might help address her issues.

"I don't believe you appreciate what Proctor Hall is. It's far more than an old farmhouse. There's more to it than Noah Proctor and his family, or Marguey Slattery, or the things people claim to see there at night. I sense things other people don't. As a result, the aura surrounding some buildings repulses me. Proctor Hall is one of the worst I've experienced.

"That said, set up a meeting if you wish, and include Marisol and Michael. I doubt a discussion will change anything, but I'm willing to listen. Maybe we can all learn something."

Everyone gathered at Channel Nine's French Quarter studio the next afternoon. The students had never been inside a television station, and they found it fascinating. So did their professor, who marveled at the amount of equipment it took just to air the six o'clock news.

Forewarned about April's concerns, Landry asked Henri to join them. His decades of experience in the paranormal field might just bring the girl around. Landry presented as straightforward and honest a case for continuing as possible.

When he finished, Henri took April aside for a private conversation. As they rejoined the others, he said, "April

THE PROCTOR HALL HORROR

agrees to go back. At the first sign of trouble, I'll take her away. But I'm hoping we can learn what happened to Andy and the secrets of Proctor Hall."

After the students and Julien left, Landry invited Henri to the Carousel Bar at the Monteleone Hotel for a cocktail. "It's five o'clock somewhere," he quipped, and Henri commented as busy as the bar always was, it might just be five o'clock in New Orleans too by the time they got their drinks.

Henri complimented Landry for his professionalism and concern for the welfare of others. Landry considered the times he'd showed neither, but he appreciated Henri's efforts to keep the project going.

He replied, "Thanks for whatever you did to change April's mind. What was the tipping point that caused that to happen?"

"April revealed something important. Not only is she a clairvoyant, she's into Ouija boards. I piqued her interest by saying being inside a haunted house with a Ouija board would be a first in my career. Who knows what the spirits may reveal?"

"Bravo," Landry said, raising his glass to clink with Henri's. "Good luck to all of us."

CHAPTER SEVENTEEN

Why do they make me stay where it's always dark? I like the light, but they won't allow it. I would like to see, but in the darkness there is nothing to see.

I don't know where I am. It is very, very quiet around me, so I must be somewhere all alone. It's a small place. I lie here; I can touch the sides, the top and bottom, but I don't tap on them. They don't like it when I do that. If I am thirsty or hungry, I wait. They will come eventually. They always have.

It's always damp, but now some water has begun to seep in. I wonder why, and if it gets worse, will it drown me?

I think about what would happen if someone didn't come. How quickly would I die? Perhaps I'm already dead, and I would just stay here forever.

CHAPTER EIGHTEEN

Landry fought to keep the Jeep in its lane as wind whipped across the interstate. They hadn't planned for a storm, but one was in their future. Born in Mexico's Campeche state, that morning tropical storm Emily had made landfall in Terrebonne Parish. Sixty-mile-an-hour winds didn't faze residents of south Louisiana — even Category 1 hurricanes didn't make most residents pack up and leave — but flooding could be an issue.

The forecasters projected Emily would turn east toward Mississippi, but storms sometimes had other plans. During the day the path shifted to the west, and now Lafourche Parish was preparing for a lot of wind and rain.

As Landry's hands clenched the wheel, Henri wondered out loud if they should have cancelled. Landry said no way, reminding him how much preparation had gone into this. A full camera crew had been at the house all day, setting up equipment, and Cate's father, Doc Adams, had flown in yesterday to watch the proceedings at the old farmhouse he'd purchased not long ago.

BILL THOMPSON

He and Cate were in the back seat, and both agreed that the show must go on. Doc said a little rain never hurt anyone, just as a jagged bolt of lightning struck a tree fifty yards off the highway that exploded with a bang.

Landry had asked Julien and the students to come by seven, which should have given them an hour to prep before sundown, but the storm changed all that. Landry had used headlights since they left New Orleans, and now at five thirty, it was dark.

He turned off the highway, splashing through huge puddles as he drove down the slick one-lane road. He lost control for a moment, sliding as Cate yelled for him to slow down. He put the Jeep in four-wheel drive and made the rest of the drive with no problem.

Landry wondered how the road would be a few hours from now. The plan was to leave the house around midnight, but if this kept up, they might have to wait for the ground to dry. That meant morning, which meant spending the night at Proctor Hall.

Cate wondered if Julien's vehicle was all-wheel drive, and Landry called to ask. The evening would be wasted without April, and if Julien's car couldn't make it to the house, everyone had assembled for nothing.

Julien said he was in his Toyota Corolla and not far out. Landry suggested he park off the highway and he'd pick them up. Cate gave her dad a tour of the old house while Henri assembled the tools that would detect fluctuations in energy levels, pick up sounds, and shoot video in infrared.

After Landry, Julien and the students hung up their drenched jackets, Landry gathered everyone in the kitchen and explained what they'd be doing. Starting with the entry hall, they would go room by room, upstairs and down. A motion-activated camera stood in each room and hallway, ready to capture any sound or movement. As lead cameraman, Phil would stay with April, recording her every move and comment as she walked from room to room.

Landry wanted to pay special attention to three areas: the stairway where Noah Proctor sat; the room where they found the bodies; and the upstairs bedroom where he and Henri found Andy Arnaud babbling about a body in the bed.

April perked up. "Which bedroom was it? The far one on the left?"

Landry nodded.

She said to Cate, "That's the room! That's where I sensed things last time. It's the most haunted room of them all. I didn't realize that's where Andy was. I can't go there. None of us can. There's something wicked in there. Something terrible."

At that moment Henri entered the room wearing a one-piece black outfit with a zipper down the front. Antennas protruded everywhere from his oversized backpack. Hoses that snaked around his torso were attached to his wrists with Velcro. There were smiles and a few titters of laughter from the assemblage. Even the stoic April smiled.

Unconcerned about his odd appearance, he tromped through the room like an astronaut on a lunar walk. Henri asked, "I heard you say one room is most haunted. Which is it?"

She told him about the upstairs bedroom, and he said he'd be by her side every step of the way, adding, "You're correct about the supernatural phenomena in this house. I've sensed a presence since the moment I stepped over the threshold. You and I will stand together against whatever it is. If you're finished here, Landry, I'd like to get started."

"There could be an army by my side and I'm still not going in there," April muttered.

They walked into the hall, Landry's director and the other WCCY-TV crew members fanning out to their stations. Just then the power failed, and the sudden darkness was so absolute it was like being in a tomb.

The director said, "Don't move until your eyes adjust. We don't want anyone running into the equipment. Guys, get the battery packs from the van."

Three men donned slickers and rushed out to retrieve the batteries while Henri, Landry and Cate took out pocket flashlights. Soon the hallways and rooms were lit again, this time from stage lights mounted high on tripods. Light bouncing off the gauzy old sheers that covered the windows created ghostly shadows that danced upon the walls.

Marisol said dramatically, "People gather in a haunted house as a storm rages outside. Then the power goes out. Is it the storm, or is Noah Proctor roaming the halls once again, wielding his bloody hatchet and looking for his next victim?"

"Stop it!" April shouted. "This is nothing to joke about. Don't you sense their presences?"

"Who? We're the only ones here, April. Just because you're the star tonight doesn't mean we need your theatrics."

April shuddered as a deep, mournful sigh echoed through the upper parts of the old farmhouse. Julien said, "We have important work to do here. Marisol, please keep your comments to yourself. Three horrific murders happened in this house, and the dead deserve our respect."

The director gave a signal, and Landry started his monologue. He gave the date and time, the names of those present and what tonight's mission would be. Then the evening's work began.

"Let's go to the sitting room," Henri said as he led everyone to that fateful chamber. In front of the fireplace stood a card table and two folding chairs the crew had set up. Henri removed his bulky pack and took a chair.

"April, please sit here across from me. Everyone else, stand back to give us space. Is there anything you can tell me about this room? What are your sensations?"

"Uneasy. Nervous. Terrified, if you want the truth."

April unzipped her backpack, removed something and put it on the table. There were murmurs from those watching as they realized what she brought out.

An old wooden Ouija board and a planchette.

"This is something new for me," Landry said into the camera as April and Henri spoke in whispers. "In my paranormal investigations I've never seen someone use a Ouija board, nor am I convinced it's anything but a parlor game. April claims to have psychic powers and has used the board, and Henri asked her to bring it along tonight. He will call out the letters if a spirit moves the pointer, and we'll see what happens."

A rolling boom of thunder shook the walls as the two rested their fingers lightly on the planchette. April said, "Is my name April?"

Nothing happened, and she asked again.

Nothing.

"Sometimes it takes a few minutes to get things going," she murmured. "Sometimes there's nobody to hear the question. But that's not right tonight, is it? There is someone here. Who are you?"

The planchette slid across the board, surprising even Henri and April, who leaned in closer to keep their fingers on the pointer.

M-E.

"ME. That's your name?"

The planchette jerked to the top of the board and paused over the word *NO*.

"Who are you, then?"

ME.

"Okay," April continued. "You're 'me.' Did you live in this house?"

NOW.

"You live here now?"

YES.

"Are you dead?"

YES.

Henri whispered to April, "No one knows where the Proctor bodies are. See if she will tell you where she's buried."

THE PROCTOR HALL HORROR

"She may not be female — or a Proctor."

"Perhaps we can find that out too."

April said, "Are you a woman?"

N-O-T-Y-E-T.

"A girl, then?"

YES.

"Is your last name Proctor?"

The planchette spun wildly, moving so quickly Henri had trouble calling out the letters.

M-Y-H-O-U-S-E

MY HOUSE.

"This is your house?"

YES.

"Where are you buried?"

HERE.

"Are you buried in this room?"

HOUSE.

"Somewhere in the house?"

YES.

"Who killed you?"

No answer.

Henri said, "Maybe she wasn't killed. We don't know who she is; she may not be a Proctor at all, and she might have died another way."

"Did you and your family die?"

DIE.

"You died. Did someone hurt you?"

YOU. DIE.

April screamed and jumped out of her chair, tossing the board and planchette to the floor. She ran out of the room, narrowly avoiding a collision with a Channel Nine cameraman. Henri caught up with her as she fumbled to unlatch the outside door. The others ran to the hall behind them, wondering what was up.

"April, wait! Everything's all right."

"I'm going to die. You saw the message!"

"I don't think that's what it meant. We haven't even established who we're talking to. Don't be afraid. We're all here with you."

"But you can't protect me. You know how this works. No one can protect me."

"Please come back. Let me ask the questions for a bit."

Reluctant, she gave in and returned. As she placed her fingers on the planchette, she cried, "Did you feel that? Something shocked me!"

THE PROCTOR HALL HORROR

Henri hadn't, perhaps because he wasn't touching the wooden instrument. He put four fingers on it, and she did the same.

He said, "ME, are you here with us?"

After a moment the planchette moved to the top of the board. *YES.*

"Is your name Proctor?"

No answer.

"How did you die?"

DIE. HOUSE.

"Did someone want you to die?"

YES.

"Who was that person?"

CRAZY.

"Someone who's crazy?"

YES.

"What's his name?"

Silence.

"Can you tell me what his name is?"

NO.

The pointer moved from letter to letter, and the answer surprised Henri.

N-O-T-H-I-M.

NOT HIM.

Did the spirit mean Noah, the one everybody believed murdered his family? Or did she mean something else?

CHAPTER NINETEEN

Henri took his fingers off the pointer and asked April to do the same. To Landry he said, "What do you make of this?"

"Perhaps the spirit's telling us Noah isn't the killer."

"You may be right, but from what little we know, it's impossible to draw a conclusion. This spirit hasn't identified herself. She considers Proctor Hall her house, meaning she might be one of the dead family members. But that may not be correct. When a lost spirit is trapped in a home, they sometimes call it their own. That may be the case here.

"The spirit says a person she calls CRAZY killed her. It's a nickname, perhaps, or a word the spirit used in life to describe the killer. She didn't say how CRAZY killed the spirit. Was it murder or perhaps an accident?"

To April he said, "We'll continue talking with the spirit later, but for now let's sign off and go exploring."

They touched the planchette and April said, "Thank you for talking to us. We'll come back later."

BILL THOMPSON

A-N-D-Y-G-O-N-E.

As Henri recited the last letter, Landry said, "What? Andy gone?"

April asked the spirit what she meant by that, but the seconds ticked by with no response. "She's left us for now," she said as Landry walked away and pulled out his cell phone. Henry gathered the others for a walking tour of the house.

When Landry returned, he caught Cate's eye and motioned for her and Doc to come into the hall. "Andy Arnaud has vanished," he said. "That's what the spirit meant."

Cate was amazed that a Ouija board told them that.

"I called the sheriff and asked how he was getting along. He said Andy disappeared from his house in Baton Rouge a couple of nights ago. He'd been doing okay, gradually regaining his memory and recalling events. His mother checked on him around ten p.m. and found his bed empty. Their surveillance camera caught him crawling out a bedroom window and running away. Nobody's heard from him since."

Doc asked, "How was he dressed? Did he have money, credit cards, a phone — things he'd need?"

"I didn't ask. The sheriff said the cops in Baton Rouge filed a missing persons report as a courtesy to his parents, but they aren't actively searching for him. He's twenty-two years old and left on his own, so there isn't much they can do. The sheriff only found out because one of the Baton Rouge cops remembered Andy's mental issues began at Proctor Hall. The cop asked Lafourche Parish deputies to keep an eye out in case he was heading back here."

THE PROCTOR HALL HORROR

Cate was skeptical, although she'd seen it with her own eyes. As Henri led the others into the hall, she asked how it was possible the board told them about Andy.

"What about Andy?" he asked.

Landry explained, and Henri rubbed his chin, deep in thought. "We must be careful," he said at last. "There are powerful negative forces at work in that upstairs bedroom where we found Andy. I think it's luring him back here. Regardless, we're on dangerous ground."

To the others he said, "Stay alert, everyone. There are paranormal phenomena everywhere in this house. We can't imagine how our intrusion affects them. Watch out for yourselves, and give a shout if you need help."

April shuddered. The man was right. The evil at Proctor Hall was the reason she'd resisted coming back. But now here she was. Here they all were, and there was nothing they could do to stop the malevolent things in this house.

CHAPTER TWENTY

The old woman hid in the trees and observed the activity. She saw the first van arrive — the one from the TV station — and as they carried equipment into the house, she wondered what they planned to do. When the rain got heavy, she took shelter in the abandoned supervisor's house a hundred yards west of Proctor Hall. Mike was the last supervisor to live there, and he'd been gone fifty years.

It was raining like the dickens when some other cars drove up to the house. She counted the people — eighteen in all. She would remember that number in case she needed it.

A little later she got a scare when the house went dark, the door flew open, and men ran out into the rain.

Are they coming over here? Did they see me looking out the window?

She crouched, ready to flee into the secret room. They'd never find her there, but after a moment she realized they had something else to do. They moved heavy boxes from the van to the house, probably batteries. Even though the power was out, soon dim lights glowed from the first-floor windows.

She hadn't seen so many lights over there in years. Usually there would be just that one light, when the ones who inhabited Proctor Hall moved about. A single light would pass across the upstairs windows as a lamp was carried from room to room. The woman had always wondered why they walked around like that, but Ben told her never to go upstairs when they did that. They didn't like intruders.

Tonight she wondered why the people came. When the rain slowed a little, she put a trash bag over her head and darted across the yard to peek through the sitting room window. A man and a girl sat at a table doing something while the others stood behind them. It was hard to see; she rubbed the vapor from her breath off the window and saw them using a Ouija board.

Idiots! What on earth do they think they're doing? They're in danger. Proctor Hall is no place to go talking to phantoms. Can't get you anywhere but in deep trouble.

Frantic, the woman wondered what to do. Ben always told her, but he wasn't here. Neither was Noah, not that he would have offered an opinion. She had to do this alone.

Should I burn down the house with them inside?

That was a foolish idea. It was raining buckets. You couldn't start a fire in a thunderstorm.

I can kill them.

No, that wouldn't work either. How would she get all those people to be still and wait while she killed them off one by one?

THE PROCTOR HALL HORROR

Every time she became frantic, her mind veered in the wrong direction. *Calm down*, she told herself as she ran back to Mike's old house. She wished Ben were here to guide her. She fretted about it for a bit longer, seeing one room grow dim and another brighten up as they moved their equipment from room to room.

Don't go upstairs, she commanded them in her head, but after an hour they did just that. They started in the bedrooms at the back, but she knew that before long they'd go to the rooms that overlooked Bayou Lafourche. They'd go to *that* room.

Ben! Ben, help me! We can't let them go in there! What if they use that Ouija board?"

Ben can never help you again, she told herself, so she made up her own mind what to do. She had to act quickly. Not only did she worry about the Ouija board, they were interrupting her nocturnal routine.

The woman knew every square inch of Proctor Hall — how to get in and move about without anyone realizing she was there. She'd go inside, take care of business, and decide what to do about all those people.

The rain pelted her as she ran across the yard and hunched down to pass through the small opening to the crawl space under the house. She could almost stand up under there. Like so many others, Proctor Hall stood on stilts to prevent flooding when the bayou overflowed. Most times the soil was dry, but tonight she slogged through several inches of water to reach the brick base of the fireplace.

The woman felt along the floorboards above her head until her fingers closed around a steel pin. She pushed on a board, tugged the pin, and as it slid out, a hinged trapdoor fell open. The opening was dark until she pushed away the corner of a rug that covered it from above. Now there came a dim glow from lights they had set up in the hallway. She entered the music room under the grand piano, removed her boots and dropped them into the muddy water below. With the door closed and the rug replaced, she listened and learned which upstairs room they were in.

She peeked into the hall, but no one was there. Everyone had gone upstairs now. It was safe to go to the kitchen. Careful not to make noise, she opened the pantry and took out a few things.

It was exciting having people in the house again after all this time. It was exhilarating to think one of them might unexpectedly discover her.

If that happened, I could kill him!

The idea made her smile, but she shouldn't think like that. There were too many of them. If they captured her, then what would happen?

She put the things from the shelves into a bag and shuffled down the hall to the music room and the trapdoor. No one in the house looked out the windows. If they had, they'd have seen an old crone moving quickly across the yard toward the trees. She was carrying a bag and looked like someone on a mission.

And that was correct. It was feeding time.

CHAPTER TWENTY-ONE

Henri's instruments recorded "energy" — not a measure of work as in physics, but a sign of paranormal activity. As he and April walked through the house, the devices recorded energy fields that should corroborate what she sensed.

Landry thought the night had been a success so far. Henri's equipment recorded dozens of energy manifestations, proof that several entities haunted the old farmhouse. In places where the readings were strongest, April's fear matched his measurable data.

She sensed far more than the instruments could detect. As they moved from room to room, she reported several entities, most of whom accepted their presence. Two were different; from them April sensed a chilling, overpowering negativity and a sense of foreboding.

"Evil things are in some rooms," she said. "When we go there, something in my head says, 'Get out! Get out!' and I know they'll hurt us if we don't."

Cate stayed by her side, providing calm reassurance as the girl's emotions ran the gamut. Landry and Henri tried to bolster her confidence too, but even they sensed a foreboding that draped the old house like a curtain.

The two primary sources of energy on the first floor surprised no one. The fourth riser of the stairway and the sitting room caused the dials to fluctuate wildly. April termed them sad and depressing.

Cate wondered what would happen in the upstairs bedroom where April had earlier experienced powerful feelings. Her job was to watch out for the girl despite Landry and Henri's push for answers. She recalled her own horrifying experience at an old French Quarter building where a murderous, long-dead spirit killed a woman named Tiffany. She knew Landry cared about April's safety, but his driving passion was the supernatural. She must choose when the session ended.

With the first floor done, the crew dismantled equipment and moved everything upstairs. They set up lights and cameras in the hallway and four bedrooms. April trembled as she went upstairs and avoided the fourth riser where Noah had sat.

Henri led them first to the storage room in the hall that became a cell. He presumed it was meant for Noah, and hoped to learn more tonight. The upstairs yielded nothing at first — neither his instruments nor April's powers detected anything.

They entered a bedroom and April said, "Someone's here. I feel a presence — a deep sadness from a lost soul."

Henri swept the room with his instruments, but for the first time tonight, he found nothing to corroborate her statement.

"A spirit?" he asked, and she shook her head.

THE PROCTOR HALL HORROR

"Something else. There's a presence, but not a negative one like in the other places. I can't explain it — there's a difference in this room — something I can't describe. The occupant of this room was a lost soul — drifting and lonely."

"Noah," Landry whispered to Cate. "I'll bet this was his room."

April reported that a spirit was following them through the house, but the entity seemed curious about them rather than sinister.

The second bedroom yielded more unique results. April had strong sensations from entities in each room. "This is Noah's mother's room," she said. "She died in that bed. There's nothing but sadness here."

"You say it's the mother's room," Landry said. "Did the parents sleep in separate rooms?"

"Yes. The next one will be his."

Henri expected the same result this time, and he was surprised when the dials flickered wildly. April reported many things happening around them. She closed her eyes and held her fingers to her temples. "They're spinning around the ceiling! Furiously, like they're in a race. Now one's coming down. Oh God. It's with me..."

She lowered her arms to her sides and stood like a statue. "We mean you no harm," she whispered. "Who are you?" She listened and nodded. "Is this your room? Your father's? I see. Please manifest yourself and let us see you."

April's eyes flew open as a wispy film grew from the floor beside her. It rose as high as her shoulder, and it took shape, rippling as if caught in a breeze. In a moment it became a shadowy figure — a person wearing a black dress.

As it fully formed, someone shouted, "It's missing its head!"

The figure vanished and April fell to the floor. Cate rushed to her, hugging her as April sobbed, "It's so sad. It's just so, so sad."

CHAPTER TWENTY-TWO

Cate sat with April until she felt ready to continue. The first question everyone had was who the spirit was.

April said, "She's May Ellen Proctor, the twelve-year-old who died in the massacre. She's the one following us around. And whoever just shouted, please restrain yourself. I have a fragile bond with the entities. When it breaks, they sometimes won't return."

She described other spirits in this room — filmy, gauzy things that were visible only to her. "May Ellen is the primary one. We have nothing to fear from her. She's a kind, gentle child. But others are just the opposite."

They moved into the hall, preparing to visit the final bedroom and the one Landry saved for last. It was where he'd found Andy beside the bed, white-haired and babbling nonsense. April had become upset in there too and had to leave. If that happened again, the session would be over, but they would only have missed the one room.

It was time to go inside. Landry and his director stood in the hallway while the crew placed tripods, lights and sound equipment. Landry hoped things would go well for April and perhaps she and Henri might use the Ouija board in there.

April only got as far as the threshold. She would not cross over despite entreaties from Henri and Landry. Cate took the girl aside and spoke with her before returning and scolding the men.

"Of all people, you two should respect her paranormal ability. She *can't* go into the bedroom. She was willing to try, even though the room scares the bejeezus out of her. Something inside — a frightening thing — is stopping her."

April added, "I heard a man's voice in my mind, but I know it wasn't a man. It's wicked and scary. It has tolerated us until now, but if one of us goes in there, someone will die."

From the doorway, the room appeared just like the others. How would merely stepping across the threshold be fatal? None of them understood.

On previous occasions Cate and Landry had gone in — she to rescue April and he to do the same with Andy. On those days odd things had happened, but neither recalled negative sensations.

"The bedroom doesn't look scary to me," Marisol said, and the camera crew agreed.

April cried, "You don't understand. None of you does. That thing is evil. It's like an enormous black cloud that will suffocate you. The entity — this *ghost* — warned me something horrific will happen if anyone goes in that bedroom!"

"Where's Michael?" Marisol asked. "He was next to me five minutes ago. He said the room looked normal to him. God, did he go in that room?"

THE PROCTOR HALL HORROR

The moment Julien realized he was missing, he said, "He's in trouble!" and ran into the bedroom. Landry started after him, but Cate grabbed his sleeve.

"No, Landry. Call out to him, but don't you dare go inside!"

Shadows filled the dark bedroom until the crew moved cameras and lights into the doorway and turned them on. The room was flooded with light.

There were sounds, perhaps a muffled conversation, and Landry yelled, "Julien, I can't see you! Did you find Michael?"

"Dear God. Oh God, yes, I found him." Julien's head appeared through the heavy mosquito netting that hung down and covered every side of the bed.

"Are you in the bed?"

He crawled out and turned toward them, to a collective gasp.

"Julien, what happened?"

"What happened? I don't know. It's not my fault. I didn't want this!"

"Julien, you're covered in blood! Come out. Hurry!"

He didn't move, and Landry shouted, "I'm going in to get him!"

April screamed, "No! You'll be next!"

Henri and Cate pulled Landry back. "Listen to her," he said. "You might die. Whatever's in there has enormous power. My instrument readings are off the chart. April's right. The spirits in that room are hell-bent on destroying us."

"What about Julien? And Michael?"

"Paranormal energy fields this strong come in bursts, like a power surge. When it decreases, you and I will run in and get them. I'll watch the readings. Be ready; when I tell you to go, we must move before the field starts up again."

The group waited anxiously for almost two minutes while Henri looked at his dials. "It's subsiding now," he said. "Get ready, Landry. Five, four, three, two, one. Go!"

Cameras rolled as they ran to the bed. Henri took Julien's arm and led him back toward the others as Landry ripped the netting. The others couldn't see what he did, but his shout of alarm was terrifying.

Henri yelled, "Get out! The energy's rising again and you only have a few seconds!"

As he dashed to the door, Landry hit something on the floor. It rolled away as he flew through the doorway like a quarterback diving into the end zone. He fell to the floor, and Cate dropped to his side.

"Did you see Michael? Do you have to go back and get him?"

"He's in there," Landry said as tears ran down his cheeks. "He's in the bed, but we're too late to save him."

"What do you mean?"

"He's dead, Cate. He's covered in blood. Somebody...somebody..." He glanced at Julien but knew he hadn't had time to kill Michael.

THE PROCTOR HALL HORROR

Cate said, "How's that possible? He was only inside for a few minutes."

"That was long enough for somebody to do their work. The thing on the floor I hit? The thing that rolled away?"

"Oh my God!" Cate screamed. "What are you saying?"

"That was his head. I kicked it like a soccer ball."

CHAPTER TWENTY-THREE

No one would consider Lafourche Parish a hotspot of felonious activity, and news of another mysterious death at Proctor Hall got everybody's attention. From the coffee drinkers at Spahr's in Thibodaux to the mudbug fishermen in Cut Off, all people talked about was the old house, the massacre, that girl who vanished twenty years ago, and whether Noah Proctor lay in wait for his next victim.

He's at it again, residents said, vowing they wouldn't set foot on that plantation if you paid them money. It was a haunted, evil place. Everybody knew that. Kid killed his entire family — cut their damned heads off — and should have gone to the chair for it. Instead, they put him in a place where high-powered shrinks checked him out, and then he ended up right back at the house to do his deeds again.

The sheriff got a lot of pressure. The head of the state police called to say the governor sure would appreciate a quick disposition of this one. If the sheriff needed help, he'd send state cops down. That wouldn't be necessary, he said, as he was determined to solve this one without the state intervening. He put every man on the case and held daily updates.

The facts of the case were baffling. Fourteen people stood in the hall outside a bedroom while someone decapitated a college student. Interviewers talked to each witness, and their accounts matched. Their records were above reproach. A noted TV personality and his camera crew. A tenured university professor and three students. The head of a state paranormal society. A prominent Texas psychiatrist and his daughter. The sheriff compared it to an Agatha Christie novel where everybody appears honest, but one of them's a killer. One thing he knew for sure — that boy didn't kill himself.

The deputies dissected what few facts they gathered. One bedroom contained "negative energy," or so claimed a young psychic girl with a Ouija board and a man with a bunch of ghost-busting equipment. The girl said someone would die if they set foot in there. A muscular college football player ignored them and entered. Minutes later, when people realized what he'd done, a distinguished Tulane professor entered and found him decapitated in a bed.

Famous paranormal investigator Landry Drake followed, dodging some supernatural energy field. The death affected him, especially after he accidentally kicked the kid's head across the room as he ran out.

This was one hell of a strange case with a diversified cast of characters, the sheriff said. Fourteen witnesses, all standing less than twenty feet from a bed with a mattress covered in blood, saw and heard nothing except for the professor, who emerged from mosquito netting in blood-soaked clothes.

During her interview, April explained what the "entity" had told her through the Ouija board. She seemed on the verge

THE PROCTOR HALL HORROR

of tears at times and said she blamed herself. If she hadn't agreed to return and contact the spirit world, none of this would have happened.

A senior investigator interviewed Landry, and his story was the same. His interrogation lasted less than fifteen minutes.

Julien Girard wasn't as lucky. He seemed confused and claimed to remember nothing about finding the boy, even though his blood was on Julien's hands and clothes.

Every witness listened to the words, "It's not my fault. I didn't want this," but Julien didn't remember saying them. The medical examiner believed he was in shock. People who observed horrific events — or did them — sometimes experienced temporary amnesia. It was the brain's way of coping with the situation.

The sheriff asked Julien to come to his office in Thibodaux that afternoon. Trembling, he asked if they were going to arrest him and worried he would lose his job at the university. He begged the officers to believe him.

The sheriff said if there was nothing to hide, there was also nothing to fear.

As an active crime scene, Proctor Hall buzzed with activity. When the power came back on around midnight, the sheriff allowed the film crew to remove their lights and equipment. Officers talked to every witness again, hoping someone's story would change just slightly and give them an opening.

Around two, the cops finished with them, and Landry drove Henri, Cate and Doc back to New Orleans. Henri fell asleep in seconds; Landry was dead tired too and thankful the rain had subsided to a few sprinkles. Cate's dad offered to drive, but Landry said he'd be fine.

Cate said, "How could someone kill Michael in the bed minutes after we saw him? As big as he was, couldn't he stop them? They decapitated him, for God's sake. He would have fought like crazy. Surely we would have heard something."

Landry hoped the authorities would find something to explain it, but he also reminded them the house was haunted. April's Ouija board experience had revealed an entity buried somewhere inside. The spirit called it "my house" and therefore might have been a Proctor. He hadn't turned up any burial records for the family. Could one still be in the house?

Doc said, "We haven't even begun to unravel the secrets, but because we started looking, a boy is dead. If we hadn't gone tonight, or if Julien Girard hadn't given an assignment to those three kids, or if they hadn't chosen the house — Michael would be alive right now. I feel responsible."

"Dad, you're looking at it backwards," Cate said. "If Michael hadn't gone off on his own, he'd be alive. April told us not to go in the bedroom, and Landry tried to keep Julien out. Everything you brought up explains how the awful thing happened, but we didn't do it."

Landry said, "It's a tragic loss. It's incomprehensible how we went from exploring the house to a brutal murder in seconds. Whoever did this is copying the Proctor Hall Massacre. It might be the same killer, but the math doesn't support it. That person would be too old to decapitate a muscular young man. Even Noah Proctor doesn't fit. He was fourteen in 1963 when his family was murdered. He was never charged, but even if he murdered them, and he's been back at the house since the eighties, he'd be well over seventy years old.

"Who killed Michael — something supernatural or a living person who's hiding there? We must go back when we can,

THE PROCTOR HALL HORROR

because it may be up to us to learn how Michael died. The cops have to look at it pragmatically. They can't consider the paranormal as a possibility, but we can. Doc, it's your house. I want permission to go back to Proctor Hall."

"We're all tired," Doc said as they passed the Superdome. "Let's get some sleep and talk in the morning."

Three miles behind Landry's Jeep, Marisol was at the wheel of Julien's Toyota. Eyes closed, April sat next to her, and Julien was curled up in the back seat, trying to sleep. Exhausted and grateful he wasn't in jail right now, he had accepted Marisol's offer to drive.

He had to be at the sheriff's office in Thibodaux that afternoon. There would be tough, intense questions about things that had no logical answers. This time he had gone too far. Despite knowing the potential danger, over the years he'd encouraged dozens of students to poke around there. They saw unexplainable phenomena — how could they not have? — but none discovered the story behind the hauntings.

"Dr. Girard, April, it's time to wake up," Marisol said as she pulled into the campus parking lot where they'd met up earlier. She asked April if she was okay walking to her dorm from here.

She nodded and gathered her things. "I'm exhausted. I just want to get some sleep now."

Marisol walked to her apartment a block from campus. She was tired, but her mind raced. How awful it had been — but how exciting at the same time — to be involved in a mystery that defied explanation. She didn't know Michael before becoming his teammate, and although she was saddened at the tragic loss of life and how it happened, she was eager to learn more. Landry Drake wouldn't stop now, and she vowed to be by his side when he went back to Proctor Hall.

CHAPTER TWENTY-FOUR

While Julien drove to Thibodaux for his meeting with the sheriff, Cate, Landry and Doc sat in Henri's office on Toulouse Street that occupied the second floor of a haunted French Quarter building featured in Landry's most recent *Bayou Hauntings* television documentary.

They came to discuss what was next for Proctor Hall. At noon, Cate had received a call from the parish sheriff. The cops had finished but had no way to lock up. Landry said he'd take care of it.

After a night's sleep, Doc said he was open to further investigation at the house but wondered if it was worth the risk. Henri said he'd analyzed the data he'd collected, and his instruments recorded levels of paranormal energy unlike any he'd seen. He hoped to return and conduct more research.

Doc smiled. "How about you, Landry? I'll bet your opinion is the same as Henri's. More investigating, more camera crews, more everything until we figure it out."

He nodded. "You know me well."

"When are you thinking of going back?" Doc asked, and Henri said the sooner the better. Paranormal activity levels fluctuated over time, and they understood how intense things were at the moment. "I wonder if April's up for another Ouija board session," he added.

Cate said, "Henri! I'm surprised at you. Would you put her through that again?"

"For the sake of saving others? Yes, I would."

Doc asked how he'd ensure her safety, and Henri replied, "Not to sound flippant, but I can't ensure my safety when I walk out on Royal Street. At any point, half the people driving in the Quarter wouldn't pass a breathalyzer. Of course we must be careful. We need April at Proctor Hall because she's our conduit to the other world. I'm confident we can conduct another session without undue risk."

Cate disagreed, Landry said Henri sounded more like him every day, and Doc said he'd go along with whatever the experts recommended. The majority ruled, and Landry asked if Cate would contact April about going back.

She rolled her eyes. "Seriously, Landry? Hell no, I won't. I'm the only one here who thinks this is a bad idea. Henri, you ask her. I'll be there to help you guys when you get in trouble, but I'm not burdening my conscience by asking her to go back after what happened."

Henri said, "Get her contact information for me, please. I'll make the call."

Sixty miles to the southwest, Julien Girard sat in an interrogation room. Across the table were the senior investigator from earlier and another cop. The investigator introduced him as Lieutenant Harry Kanter and said he would run today's interview.

THE PROCTOR HALL HORROR

Julien hadn't expected to see the state police involved, and he asked why. Kanter explained, "Parish authorities ask us for help on special situations and unusual cases. I think you'd agree this one qualifies on both counts."

Kanter seemed good-natured, but Julien warned himself to be careful. This man wasn't his friend. He was here to solve a crime, one that Julien was in the big middle of.

After a few preliminary questions, the lieutenant asked about Julien's connection with Landry Drake. It was an easy answer. They both knew a man named Henri Duchamp, through whom he'd met Landry a few weeks ago.

Kanter asked where they met, and Julien replied it was at Proctor Hall. He described their first meeting and how he'd joined Landry and Henri for a tour of the property.

"Let me be sure I understand. You're saying you never met Landry Drake prior to your recent introduction to him at Proctor Hall?"

"That's correct."

"Does the name Andrew Arnaud mean anything to you?"

Andy? "Uh, sure. Andy is — was, I should say — one of my students."

"And why do you say he *was* a student?"

"Because…because of what happened to him. He had some kind of psychotic episode and wasn't able to return to school."

"And where did he have this episode?"

"At Proctor Hall."

"You have vast knowledge about that old house, don't you, Dr. Girard? Would it be fair to say you're an authority on it?"

Julien stumbled on his reply. "I wouldn't go that far. I find the stories fascinating, so I've spent time researching it. For my classes on Louisiana culture, that is. There are a lot of things that happened there —"

Kanter interrupted. "Like the Proctor Hall Massacre and a girl who disappeared in the nineties? Are those the kinds of things you're referring to?"

In a subtle shift, the cop's tone had gone from cordiality to a no-nonsense line of questioning that was intrusive and harsh. He struggled to avoid making a mistake. "I was referring to the paranormal things people claim to have experienced," he answered.

Kanter closed the tablet on which he'd been taking notes and said, "Dr. Girard, I want you to take a ride with me. Up to headquarters in Baton Rouge. I'd like you to submit to a polygraph examination. It's strictly voluntary. You can say no, but often clearing the air on things helps both of us. If everything goes well, I'll have you back here by six."

A lie detector? Chills went down Julien's spine. He'd heard horror stories about innocent people getting flustered and flunking a polygraph.

"Before I agree, I'd like to know why you want it and if I need to call a lawyer."

"You claim to remember nothing about lying in a bed with a decapitated body, your clothes and hands covered in the victim's blood. You're a respected member of the academic community, Dr. Girard, and perhaps there's a reasonable

THE PROCTOR HALL HORROR

explanation about your involvement. I just can't figure out what it is, and you can't remember enough to help me. Or so you claim.

"I'm requesting a polygraph to be sure you've given us accurate information. You're free to contact an attorney, although one cannot be present with you when the polygraph is administered. You're not under arrest, although as we gather evidence, that could change. I'm sure you understand that."

He gulped. "What if I decide I'd rather not take the polygraph?"

"If you have nothing to hide, then you also have nothing to fear. You have a lot to explain, sir, and so far you can't remember anything. A polygraph helps us decide whether you're forgetful or you're hiding things. So if you turned me down, I'd go to the DA. He'll say we have probable cause, we'll arrest you, and that's when you'd be needing that attorney you mentioned."

Julien had no choice but to cooperate. Neither spoke as he and the lieutenant rode to Baton Rouge and entered a small room on the third floor of the state police building. *Be calm. Just be calm,* he said to himself as a female officer attached a pressure cuff, straps and connectors to his torso and fingers.

His voice cracked when he said, "I'm so nervous, there's no way I can pass this."

"Don't worry, sir. It happens to everyone. The machine compensates for anxiety." She sat at a desk across from him and explained how things would work. There would be control questions — verifiable ones like his age and occupation. Others were moral questions — "Have you ever stolen anything?" "Have you ever wished you could kill another person?" His answers to these would establish a basis to evaluate the direct questions about Michael's murder.

Julien held his breath for a moment, forced a total exhale, and steeled himself. He'd faced problems before, and he knew how to control his emotions. If there was ever a time to steady his nerves, this was it.

The examiner asked questions in a steady, even tone, and Julien paused before answering even the most basic of them. He willed himself to take things easy, think before answering, and offer a simple yes or no.

After thirty minutes, she told him it was over, unhooked him, and asked him to wait for Lieutenant Kanter to return.

"Just tell me — did I pass?"

"Most of your answers were inconclusive. That means the machine couldn't determine their veracity. No, Dr. Girard, you didn't pass. But you didn't fail either."

"So am I free to go?"

"Please wait here for Lieutenant Kanter." She turned and left him alone in the little room for fifteen minutes. Julien imagined the two of them going over his answers, and he wondered if "inconclusive" meant freedom or jail. Soon he found out.

Kanter walked in and snapped, "Let's go."

"Where?"

"Back to Thibodaux, where your car is."

They rode in silence until they were close to the sheriff's office. Kanter said, "People react to polygraph examinations in many ways. The innocent ones do the

THE PROCTOR HALL HORROR

worst. They sweat bullets, answer questions too fast, get wordy — that kind of stuff. Other people sit there without emotion, give answers designed to confuse the machine, and think they've outwitted the system. Today you looked like the second kind, Dr. Girard, but for now you're free to go. I want you to keep something in mind. I'm going to spend every hour of my time working to solve that kid's murder. As you go through each day, think about me. If you're innocent, you have nothing to worry about. If you're not, you'd better sleep with one eye open, because I'll get you eventually."

Julien gulped. "Are you threatening me?"

"No, sir. Not at all. I've been in this business for years. In my experience, people with nothing to hide don't answer questions like you did this afternoon. You just gave me a little more work to do, that's all. Here we are. Have a good week."

He walked to his car on wobbly knees, the tension gone at last. As he started the engine, his body relaxed for the first time in hours.

It was over. For the moment.

Julien opened the car door, leaned out, and threw up.

CHAPTER TWENTY-FIVE

April listened to Henri explain why they must return to Proctor Hall so they might learn how and why Michael died. She understood how the Ouija board might help, but she also appreciated Henri's ulterior motive. Michael's death wasn't the only thing he and Landry Drake were keen to solve.

"We don't have to do the Ouija board at the house," she said. "We can ask the same questions right here on campus, and it will answer."

"My plan is to use more than just the board this time. I want to go up a notch. Let's conduct a seance."

"I've never had the nerve to do that," she said. "I discovered my psychic abilities using the board, but to me a seance is way more than going up a notch. Have you ever seen one?"

Henri said he had attended three over the years. One was pure fakery, another was a dud — nobody was home on the other side — and during the third, they contacted a spirit. At least it seemed so to Henri, who admitted he wasn't a believer in seances. To him it was more likely things happened because of energy emissions from the persons around the table than otherworldly entities.

April said, "What worries me about conducting one at Proctor Hall is the evil entities there, especially in that one bedroom. I contacted a spirit last time we were there, but we never established if she was friendly. I don't want to create problems for me or anybody else. What if we learned the hard way seances are real? What if we opened a passageway to the other side and let even more evil things in?"

Henri explained that sometimes spirits cannot rest or break free from whatever bonds tie them to a place. In his experience, contacting them often gave them the peace they so desperately sought. He wasn't asking to do a seance in the bedroom. Instead, he planned to set up a table in the hallway just outside the door.

"The door Michael entered but never came out of. You can't be sure something awful won't happen."

Henri wanted to learn the secrets while being honest with her. "That's correct. No one can guarantee what will happen when one ventures into that world. We can take precautions to minimize the danger, but there will be a risk. I'm willing to sit beside you and find out what's behind the mysteries. So are Landry and Cate and her dad. We'll all be there together. Please allow us to try."

She thought for a moment and said, "I don't like all those guys with cameras and lights and stuff. Not only is it distracting, I feel like they're crawling into my soul."

"Okay. One guy with a video camera. No lights, no wires everywhere. Will you do it?"

"I want Marisol there. And Dr. Girard."

THE PROCTOR HALL HORROR

"If I can get them to come along, will you go back?"

"I don't want to. My better judgment is screaming 'No!' But for the sake of getting answers, and because you need me, I'll do it. Please, Mr. Duchamp. Please keep us all safe."

"I'll do my best," he said. In one respect, he was glad she consented, but he shared her fears about the place.

A few days later they were at the house again. Phil was the lone cameraman this time, and that suited Landry. They had worked together for so long, Phil could anticipate what Landry would do next. He hadn't failed to capture an important shot yet.

Henri had left behind what they called his space suit, opting this time for an array of instruments he arranged in the upstairs hallway and bedroom. The energy from what they now called the haunted bedroom registered zero, and he worried that they might not raise a spirit today. He asked that the lights be off; the only illumination came through the windows at either end of the hall. The eerie half-light created just the scene he wanted.

As the others watched, Henri and April sat at a table in the hallway with the Ouija board between them. They placed their fingers on the planchette, and Henri said, "ME. Are you here?"

Nothing happened, and he called for the entity again. Still no response.

April tried. "Hello. We've come back to visit again. Will you talk to us?"

Nothing for a moment, and then the planchette moved up to the word *YES*.

"You said you were ME, but it wasn't your name. What is your name?"

ME.

"Is that a nickname?"

YES.

"What's your actual name?"

M-A-Y-E-L-L-E-N

Henri raised his eyebrows and glanced at Landry. This was a breakthrough. "Let me speak for a moment," he whispered to April.

"Are you May Ellen Proctor?"

YES.

"You said earlier you're buried in this house. Where is your body buried?"

T-A-L-K-T-O-H-E-R.

April said, "Okay, I'll talk to you. Where are you buried?"

HOUSE.

"What room?"

No answer.

"The person who killed you. The one you call Crazy. Is that Noah?"

THE PROCTOR HALL HORROR

The planchette almost flew out of their hands as it created the answer letter by letter.

CRAZY.

"I don't understand your answer, May Ellen."

CRAZY.

Henri said, "Let's try a seance now." They cleared the table, and he brought out three candlesticks that held purple candles, placed them in the center of the table, and lit them. Everyone except Phil stood in a circle around the table and held hands. He told April to summon Noah's sister, May Ellen, who had been twelve in 1963 when the family died.

She began by saying, "I summon only friendly spirits to our circle. Right now I reach out to May Ellen Proctor. Please make your presence visible to us."

In the half-light, the flames of the candles danced back and forth as if a breeze had arisen, although there was none.

"Are you here?"

The candles flickered more intensely, and someone spoke. It came from somewhere and nowhere — close by, at the far end of the hall, by the ceiling — it was impossible to say.

The voice echoed as if coming from somewhere deep within the walls of the house. "What is your name?"

"April. My name is April. Is it you, May Ellen?"

Without breaking the circle of clasped hands, Landry gave a hard nod to the left, where something ethereal stood just inside the bedroom. At one moment it was formless, but in the next it morphed into the shape of a girl wearing a long dress. A girl with no head.

April said, "I'm so glad to see you at last. Thank you for coming here."

I'm sad.

"I understand. Your death was tragic and horrible."

Sad for you.

"For me? Why would you feel sad for me?"

CRAZY is here.

"The person who killed your family. That is sad. Tragic."

CRAZY is here. Danger for you. I'm sad.

April jerked her hands away from Henri and Cate. The candles stopped flickering, and the entity in the doorway vanished.

"This is what I was afraid of! Nobody knows what happened to Noah Proctor. What if he's still here — hiding somewhere after all these years? It's dangerous for us to be in this house! That's what May Ellen is telling me. He killed Michael just like he killed his own family and Marguey Slattery."

"We don't know that," Henri said. "You broke the circle before we found out what she meant."

"She scared me. Didn't you hear what she said? Crazy — whoever that is — Crazy is here, and that's sad for me. That can only mean one thing."

THE PROCTOR HALL HORROR

"It could mean a lot of things," Landry said. "We don't know if Crazy is a ghost or a living person. If what she's saying is right — and spirits don't always tell the truth — then perhaps a live person followed us here. He could be inside the house right now. Or hiding somewhere nearby."

As April's eyes grew wide, Cate said, "Good job, Landry. You sure can ease a person's fears."

"I was just trying to convince April it could be something besides a ghost."

There was a noise — a loud thump that came from below. "I'll check it out," Julien said, flying down the stairs two at a time.

After hearing nothing, Landry yelled, "Julien! Everything okay down there?"

After a long pause, he said, "I'm not sure. I don't quite know how to explain this."

Camera in hand, Phil sprinted down first, followed by Landry, Henri and the others. Julien stood in the sitting room, pointing toward the fireplace. On the mantel where the Proctor family's heads once rested were three jack-o'-lanterns carved with grotesque, grimacing faces.

On the wall next to the mantel, someone had scribbled a single word.

CRAZY.

CHAPTER TWENTY-SIX

From that point on, they made no more attempts to contact a spirit. April curled up on the floor, moaning to herself, while Julien stared spellbound at the bizarre jack-o'-lanterns.

Cate and Marisol helped April stand and took her out to the car while Landry asked Julien what had happened when he reached the first floor.

Unsteady, Julien sat on the fateful couch, realized where he was, and jumped up with a cry of alarm. He took a straight-back chair on the other side of the room, as far from the fireplace as possible. He spoke in disjointed words, as if his thoughts were difficult to articulate.

"I looked in here to see what made the noise, because this is where most of the spirit activity is. Then…well, when I saw *them*, I just stood there. I was frozen." He pointed to the mantel.

It came as no surprise that the grotesque pumpkins shocked Julien. Two were the size of adult heads and the third smaller, like May Ellen's. Skillfully carved and frightening to behold, they were the stuff of nightmares.

"I suppose it's best to wrap things up here," Henri said, but Landry had another idea. He suggested sending Cate, Doc, Julien and April home in the Jeep, while he and Henri stayed. Phil the cameraman too — just in case something else developed.

"There are things going on here that defy explanation, like the spirit who talked to you and April. But that isn't all that's happening at Proctor Hall. A ghost didn't carve these pumpkins. There's someone else around. Let's find out where."

Doc said he appreciated Landry's wanting to ship him back to New Orleans, but he said he'd rather stay and observe. "Don't forget whose house you're in," he kidded. "If I go, we all go."

Julien also asked to stay, claiming to feel much better and wanting to see what they found, but Landry refused. He'd been through a traumatic episode, and after some half-hearted arguing, he agreed to go.

After they left, the men walked to the upstairs bedroom. Once again, Henri's monitors reported no negative energy. They walked through the doorway and across the room to the bed. Landry pulled back the sheer netting and revealed the bloodstained covers and the clear imprints of two bodies. Julien had lain next to Michael's corpse before being roused by their shouts. How had everything happened so quickly? And why?

That day Michael died and the deputies came to Proctor Hall, Landry and Henri had theorized about what happened. Henri reported high negative energy levels when Julien was in the bedroom. Did the spirits there take control of Julien's

THE PROCTOR HALL HORROR

mind? Could a phantom decapitate a person? Or was there a rational answer?

When seeking answers, Landry and Henri considered the logical possibilities before the paranormal. Today Landry asked if they thought Noah Proctor could be hiding in the house, carrying out his grisly work on strangers who dared to enter.

"Where might a person hide?" Doc asked, prompting Henri to inquire if Doc had a set of plans. He didn't, and Henri said owners often installed hiding places, nooks and crannies in old houses. Many antebellum mansions had them; Proctor Hall wasn't of that era, but perhaps it had secret places too.

"So you think it might be Noah?" Landry asked.

"Maybe, but if we limit our thinking to one possibility, we may exclude the answer. Let's have a look around."

They split up and went to work examining closets from top to bottom, moving large pieces of furniture to see what lay behind, and looking at bookshelves, cabinets and panels. On the floor, Doc found the piece of burnt wood that someone used to write the word CRAZY beside the mantel.

An hour later Henri called to them from upstairs, saying he'd found something interesting in the hallway across from the haunted bedroom. He pointed to the oak paneling that lined the upstairs and lower halls, and moved his hands up and down each side, knocking on the panels every few feet.

He asked them to listen as he rapped on the walls. Every knock resounded with a solid thump until he reached one that didn't. This one moved a little when he gave it a hard hit. It sounded hollow instead of muffled, like the others. There was an open space behind this panel.

Henri wondered how to open it, and Doc said, "Let's figure it out. If nothing else works, we can remove the panel."

Landry calculated that the kitchen lay just below, and he went there while Doc and Henri examined the panels. They'd searched the kitchen earlier, but he wondered if they had missed something. Their knocking upstairs seemed to be right above the pantry, so he started there. There were cans of food on the shelves that looked brand new, although the expiration dates were in the years prior to 2018, when the reporter found the house abandoned.

The back of the pantry was a wood-paneled wall. He stepped into the tiny room to look more closely and jumped back when the back wall silently slid to the left. There stood Doc at the bottom of a narrow, steep stairway. He stepped out with Henri close behind.

"Surprise!" Doc said. "A hidden staircase!"

Not so, Henri said, suggesting the stairs were for household servants who weren't allowed to use the main staircase. They were an easy way to access the bedrooms, and upon further examination, Henri found they continued up into a small attic room that was empty.

Landry asked how they'd found the stairway. They had been ready to tear out the panel when Henri pointed out something. Each panel was bordered on four sides by decorative molding. On this one, the panel inside the trim was actually a door. When they found the right place to push, it swung inward, revealing the stairs.

For Landry this discovery meant there could be other hidden areas that allowed people to move about unnoticed. Encouraged by their find, they rapped on panels for another hour before giving up and locking the house.

THE PROCTOR HALL HORROR

It was dusk when they left Proctor Hall. As they drove away, they started a discussion on Michael's murder and if it was related to the others. If one of them had turned to look through the rear window, he would have seen a solitary light move from room to room across the upper floor. Now that the strangers were gone, the house was theirs again.

CHAPTER TWENTY-SEVEN

Jack Blair stopped by Landry's office the next morning to ask about his trip to Thibodaux. Once Landry's unpaid assistant, Jack was now an investigative reporter for Channel Nine, and Landry was his boss. Jack had been keeping up with the goings-on at Proctor Hall, and he wanted news about the latest spirit contact.

Landry explained the aborted seance, the jack-o'-lanterns and the word scrawled on the wall beside the mantel, adding, "This isn't the work of some spirit. I want to find out who did this. The likely suspect is Noah Proctor, but he and his keepers abandoned the place years ago. What if someone else is making it appear Noah's still at work? The poor guy may be guilty or innocent and alive or dead by now. As far as I know, people last saw him when the Slattery girl disappeared years ago."

Jack offered to search also, and Landry said he'd appreciate it. Jack's forte was investigative research; he often turned up things others missed.

"Tell me what you're still looking for," Jack said, and Landry named them off the top of his head.

Was Noah still alive? If not, where was he buried, and his family too? Where did Ben and Agnes Trimble go? And what happened to Marguey Slattery?

He laughed. "Holy crap. I should have volunteered to help earlier. Sounds like you have more questions than answers!"

Landry called Julien Girard's office at Tulane and left a voicemail. The woman who returned the call said Julien was ill and would be out for a few days. She promised to pass along the message, and fifteen minutes later Julien called. To Landry, his voice sounded strong for someone not feeling well.

Julien said the pumpkin heads tormented him. He was taking a long weekend but would be back in the classroom on Monday. He asked if Landry had found anything interesting after they sent him back to New Orleans.

Landry told him about the stairway, and then he asked if Julien had spoken with April. He admitted he hadn't felt up to it, suggested Landry contact Marisol for an update, and gave him her email address.

Marisol said April was still frazzled by the incident. "We're meeting this afternoon to wrap up the report on Proctor Hall for Dr. Girard's class," she added. "Since April refuses to go back, I'm hoping what we've done is enough to snag the top grade. Since Dr. Girard himself was part of our research, I hope we get it."

Landry agreed no other team would have that edge. She promised to keep in touch, and then he called Henri to request a last-minute lunch to discuss what to do next.

They met at Kingfish on Conti Street, one of their favorites. The hostess showed them to a quiet table in the back. When the wine came, Landry brought Henri current, asking, "What should we do next?"

Henri said, "I understand why April says she won't go back, but that's unfortunate for our ends. I was hoping to find out what the Ouija board would tell us about that bedroom."

"I'll ask Cate to talk to April."

Henri laughed. "You're wasting your time, I'm afraid. She and I talked this morning. As much as I want answers, I worry if we can keep April safe too. The spirits warned April to stay away. If I coerced her into that room and something awful happened, it would devastate me. I daresay you agree with me."

"I do, but where does that leave us?"

"Perhaps we enlist the services of a professional spiritualist, or try it ourselves."

"How do you find spirit mediums? Do they advertise online?"

"The fake ones do, and that's the problem. New Orleans is rife with people claiming to be voodoo queens or spiritualists or palm readers. They have tables set up all around Jackson Square. How we'd find a genuine spiritualist, I don't know. I've never looked for one, but if you wish, I can make some enquiries."

They ordered lunch, and Landry asked him about trying it themselves, without a medium. How would that work?

Henri said they needed four or five people familiar with Proctor Hall's spirits. Those might be the two of them plus Cate, Doc, Julien and perhaps Marisol. They would attempt to contact a spirit just as April had done. Even without psychic powers, one of them might make something happen. After all, amateurs held Ouija board seances all the time.

Landry agreed, but he still was skeptical a Ouija board was a conduit to the spirit world. Regardless, he suggested starting by themselves. If things didn't work, they'd find a medium.

They returned to Henri's office after lunch and ran the idea by Cate, who said she had been waiting for the next shoe to drop. "You guys just can't leave a bad thing alone," she said, only half joking. "To answer your question, I think holding a seance ourselves is a waste of time since nobody's clairvoyant, but I'm game to try. I'm just glad you both came to your senses enough to leave April out of it."

As Landry left for the studio, Cate called her father to arrange another visit to Proctor Hall.

CHAPTER TWENTY-EIGHT

BUZZ ME WHEN YOU'RE BACK, read the sticky note stuck in the middle of Landry's monitor. He smiled; not that long ago, Jack Blair had been a homeless person, and now he was an enthusiastic, productive member of WCCY-TV's team.

BACK, he messaged, and seconds later Jack appeared in his doorway.

"Have you answered all my questions?" Landry asked with a grin.

"In two hours? Give me a break, okay? I'm good, but not that good. I found out about Noah Proctor. According to the records on file in Baton Rouge, Noah Proctor was born in 1949 and died on the first of October 2003, aged fifty-four."

"Seems cut and dried," Landry commented. "Where's he buried?"

"That's where things get dicey. He died at an address in a town twenty-five miles south of Proctor Hall called Lockport. The cause of death was exposure."

"Exposure to what?"

"First things first. I needed to find Frank Caparelli, the doctor who signed Noah's death certificate. I wanted to ask the doctor what 'exposure' meant. His address in Lockport is on the death certificate, but I ran into a snag."

Landry waited, but Jack just smiled. This was a game he played when he had something interesting to reveal, and it was tiresome when Landry had other things going on.

"Tell me, Jack. I have stuff to do. So do you."

"Dr. Caparelli doesn't live in Lockport."

"So what? Did he move or die or what?"

"Or what. The address on the death certificate doesn't exist."

"Maybe someone wrote the wrong address."

"But the handwriting's identical to the signature. Do you think the good doctor forgot the street and town where he lived? I checked the state database. No person by that name has ever lived in Lafourche Parish. In fact, no physician of any kind — MD, DO, chiropractor or witch doctor — named Frank Caparelli ever held a medical license in Louisiana.

"Noah Proctor's death certificate shows he's buried in the Lockport cemetery, but that's news to the people there. I spoke to the man who runs the place. Like everyone in the parish, he knows about Proctor Hall, but no Proctors are buried in Lockport.

THE PROCTOR HALL HORROR

"Noah's death certificate is a forgery, but it appears nobody picked it up. Back in 2003 somebody killed Noah off, so to speak. Sounds to me like he might be alive. Did you find out anything more?"

"No, but I agree with you he might be alive. I suggest going to Lockport and talking to the people who live in the house. I'd do it for you, but I'm in the middle of a project for the boss."

"I'll go. What's the address, and who lives there?"

Jack looked at his notes. "Yeah, I cross-checked the name and address. The place is on the west bank of Bayou Lafourche in Lockport. That would be Highway 1. Google Earth shows the house sits just feet from the water. The owners are Joseph and Mary, like in the Bible. Last name's Girard."

Landry jerked his head up. "Their last name's Girard? Are you sure?"

Jack nodded and asked why that name was significant.

Joseph and Mary Girard.

Landry had a sick feeling in his gut. This was no coincidence. They had the same last name as the professor's. It was an important discovery, but what it meant was a mystery.

Landry got little sleep that night. He tossed and turned, wondering where to begin unraveling the mystery, how Noah was involved, and who Julien really was.

CHAPTER TWENTY-NINE

It took just over an hour to drive from New Orleans to Lockport, a tiny town split down the middle by Bayou Lafourche. Highway 1 ran along the east side and 308 on the west. The occasional bridge allowed passage from one side of town to the other.

Landry found the Girard house with no trouble. It was a small clapboard, and as Jack said, it sat feet from the riverbank. He wondered about erosion. If the bank eroded or the river overflowed its banks, every house along this stretch would either be in the bayou or flooded.

The place needed work. The front porch roof sagged where a post had fallen, and the house hadn't seen paint in years. In the front yard a refrigerator lay on its side, and an old pickup with no wheels sat on blocks. Tall grass grew around the chassis, an indicator of how long it had sat there.

As Landry walked toward the house, the only sounds were the buzzing chirps of crickets and laughter coming from two boys fishing thirty feet away along the bayou. He tested the porch steps before using them, walked to a screen door, and knocked. He called Joseph's name, but no one answered.

He walked to the back, rapped on the door, and shouted, "Mr. Girard! Joseph. Mary. Is anybody home?"

"Nobody lives there, mister." The kids who'd been fishing stood in the yard now. "Those people have been gone a while."

"How long?" he asked, and the boy said he wasn't exactly sure. It could be a year.

"Where did they go?"

"You the law?" the other one asked. "Why are you asking so many questions? Did they do something bad?"

Landry smiled. "I'm not the law. I'm a friend and I came to see them."

"Didn't know they had any friends," one boy said to the other. "Did you?"

"Nope. Nobody comes around here 'cept that guy that checks on things sometimes. He isn't here long. Just goes in the house for a few minutes and leaves."

"Can you tell me what he looks like?"

"I dunno. Old guy with a ponytail. He drives a silver car."

"Toyota," the other boy said. "A Toyota Corolla, like my old man's."

Old guy with a ponytail. Silver Corolla. They're describing Julien Girard.

"How often does he come?"

THE PROCTOR HALL HORROR

"Every few weeks, I guess. He hasn't come in a while."

"If I give you my number, would you call me next time you see him?"

"We don't have a phone, mister. You sure you ain't the law?"

No amount of assurance would convince the boys. In a close-knit community, even the kids looked out for their own. He gave them each a dollar and said, "Go buy yourself something fun."

"I'm gettin' night crawlers," one said. "We've been fishin' with bologna, but the fish figured that out. You put a worm on there, they'll stand in line to get on that hook!"

Landry drove to the cemetery and found the older man who'd spoken to Jack earlier. He reiterated that the record book showed no Proctors in the cemetery's two-hundred-year history.

"What about Girard? Do you have any of them?"

"Girard. They came to Lafourche Parish in the late eighteen hundreds. They're all buried in a family plot at the Catholic cemetery in Thibodaux. May I ask why you're interested in the Girards? Since I've lived in this parish for seventy years, perhaps I can help you."

"I hoped to find Joseph and Mary Girard, but it looks like they haven't lived in the house for some time. Two boys said a man sometimes comes to check on things. Any idea where the Girards are these days?"

"No, but I heard tell they moved away. The man who comes — that's their nephew Julien."

His pulse quickened. "Julien Girard?"

"Yes. He teaches school somewhere. They considered him their son. They raised him his whole life, from when he was a little baby."

"Who were his parents?"

"Relatives from somewhere. People look after their own in these parts."

"You're sure they aren't his actual parents? He has their last name."

"Like I say, they raised him like their own, since he even had their last name."

Landry drove to the St. Joseph Cemetery in Thibodaux, found the Girard plot, and saw a dozen markers. The most recent burials had happened over twenty years ago. He found no Proctors here either. The solution to this enigma wouldn't be that simple.

As he drove back to New Orleans, he plotted his next move. The next time Julien came to Lockport, the boys would tell him someone in a Jeep Grand Cherokee came around asking a lot of questions. If Julien was up to something, he'd raise his guard and concoct a plausible story. If he hurried, he could surprise Julien and catch him unawares.

He got off the interstate at the Tulane University exit. He'd stop by Hebert Hall and drop in on Julien.

CHAPTER THIRTY

Julien smiled as Landry opened his office door. "What a surprise! To what do I owe the honor? Come in and take a seat if you can find one."

Like the proverbial absent-minded professor, Julien had a cluttered office. Stacks of books and yellow pads rose from every empty space. Julien moved some journals from a chair to the floor and motioned for Landry to sit.

"What's up? More news on Proctor Hall?"

"No, something else. I drove over to Lockport today."

Landry watched Julien's reaction. He shifted in his chair and said, "Really? What on earth took you to that tiny place?"

"Do you know it?"

He smiled. "Sure. I grew up in Lockport, and I lived there until I left for college."

"Did you know Joseph and Mary Girard?"

"Sure. They're my parents. What's this about, Landry? Is something wrong?"

He claims they're his parents. "Where are they now?"

Julien became wary. "Why all the questions? Did you go there to see them? What's going on?"

"They don't live there now, and you go there sometimes to check on the house. Where are they?"

"Hey, man, this feels like an interrogation."

"I merely asked you where your parents are. Is that a tough question to answer?"

"Not at all, and I'm happy to do it. But why the sudden change in attitude toward me? We were friends the last time I saw you, and now you're acting like you don't trust me."

"Answer the question, Julien. Where are the Girards?"

"Savannah, where my brother lives. They're in a retirement center. Now will you please tell me what's wrong?"

"Have you ever heard of a doctor in Lafourche Parish named Frank Caparelli?"

"No. Who's he?"

"Would it surprise you to learn that Noah Proctor died at your parents' house in Lockport? Or were you aware of it, and you've neglected to mention it all this time?"

Julien's demeanor changed. Now he was aggressive. "Are you nuts? I'm not sure what the hell you think you're doing, but that's preposterous. Somebody's feeding you

THE PROCTOR HALL HORROR

lies, and you're falling for them. You think I'm guilty of something — or my parents are. Where in hell are you getting your information?"

"From a public record. From Noah's death certificate. Dr. Frank Caparelli signed it, but so far it appears he doesn't exist. The address where Noah died is your house in Lockport — Joseph and Mary Girard's house. The cause of death is exposure. What does that mean, Julien? What happened to Noah at the house in Lockport? And who are the Girards? One thing's for certain — they're not your parents."

"What the hell are you doing? Get out of my office!"

"You can talk to me or the police, because if I leave here without answers, that's my next stop. Joseph and Mary have some connection to the Proctors, and that means you do too. With your help or without it, I'll find out what you're up to."

Julien's face was flushed. He shouted, "You have it all wrong and it's none of your business anyway. Stop meddling and get the hell out of my office!"

Back at Channel Nine, Landry asked Jack to bring him a copy of Noah Proctor's death certificate. In his office, he told Jack about the trip to Lockport and his bizarre confrontation with Julien Girard.

"Sounds like you touched a nerve," Jack said, and Landry agreed the guy's odd behavior and unexpected belligerence signaled something was off.

"Why would he say his aunt and uncle were his parents? What's he trying to hide?"

"Perhaps the man who told you that was wrong. He might be confused about Julien's relationship to the Girards."

Landry removed a small journal from his pocket, turned to a page filled with handwritten notes, and laid it on his desk next to the death certificate. "Julien's reaction proves he's hiding something. Let's see if this gives us any clues."

He grinned. "Just as I expected. On the death certificate, look at the entries Dr. Caparelli hand-printed — his address and name — and his signature. Do they resemble the handwriting in this book?"

"Looks like a perfect match to me. Where did you get it?"

"I pilfered it from Julien Girard's office. There's so much stuff crammed in there he'll never notice it's gone. After the way he acted, I had a hunch about this. It was my only chance, since I don't expect an invitation back anytime soon. Now that we know who created Dr. Frank Caparelli, I want to find out why he did it."

Landry's threat to go to the police was an empty one. Even if the authorities agreed that the handwriting on the forged death certificate matched what was in the stolen journal, it proved nothing.

He sat back and considered what he had learned. Was he trying too hard to connect the dots? Julien said he had the facts all wrong, and perhaps he did.

The Girards were Julien's parents…or his aunt and uncle. Did it matter which? The lady claimed they raised him from birth. So what if he called them Mom and Dad? That was no mystery. Lots of people in his situation did that.

Joseph and Mary Girard abandoned their house and disappeared. Or they moved to a retirement home in Savannah. Again, there was a logical explanation. He searched for the last name Girard in Savannah and found a hundred matches. There were two hundred retirement

THE PROCTOR HALL HORROR

centers. Without Julien's brother's first name, he was wasting his time.

CHAPTER THIRTY-ONE

April's screen flashed a number she didn't recognize. She let it go to voicemail, played it back and heard her history professor Dr. Girard ask for a return call.

When she did, he said, "Thanks for calling me back. I wondered if we could meet somewhere." She hardly recognized his voice; he sounded anxious and breathless.

"Are you all right?"

"Yes. Things have gone crazy and my life's out of control. I want to meet with you...to talk to you in person. We shared experiences at Proctor Hall, and I need someone to share my thoughts with."

She understood he might be upset about the house, but something about this call bothered her — something that just wasn't right. *He's my teacher, a single guy thirty years older than me, calling at nine p.m. asking to get together.* He said this wasn't about school. It was personal, and she was uneasy. She knew Dr. Girard from class and she liked him, but she didn't feel comfortable talking about his feelings.

"What are you asking?"

"You live on campus, right? I'll pick you up on Freret Street in front of Butler House in fifteen minutes."

"No reflection on you, but I'm not doing it that way. Tell me what this is about."

"My life. Proctor Hall. Landry Drake. Everything. I'm spinning out of control, April. That place is haunting my dreams. I can't work. I can't think. You were there; you experienced the paranormal activity. I want to talk to you about everything and find out if your thoughts and mine are the same."

April understood, because what happened had unnerved her. The jack-o'-lantern incident frightened her so much that she still couldn't sleep in the dark. She felt sorry for him, but her instincts sent danger signals.

"I'll meet you at the Boot," she offered. A popular bar a few blocks off campus, there was always a crowd. He said it would be too noisy to talk. They needed someplace quiet.

"Dr. Girard, I'll be frank. This call is making me nervous. I can't help you — I can't even help myself right now — but I'm willing to listen. If I agree to meet you, it's going to be somewhere noisy and crowded. It's the Boot or nowhere."

She arrived ten minutes earlier than he. She waved from her table and as he maneuvered through the crowd, his disheveled appearance surprised her. In sharp contrast to his classroom look, he wore a stained, untucked shirt; he was unshaven; and instead of pulling his long hair back into a ponytail, he let it hang in strands down his neck. He looked like a desperate man.

THE PROCTOR HALL HORROR

As he walked through the bar, he stopped to speak to some students before joining her. They ordered beers, and he thanked her for coming.

"I didn't mean to scare you," he began, and she said it was nothing personal, but everybody had to be careful these days.

"I think I'm having a breakdown. Proctor Hall has become my obsession, and today Landry Drake came around asking questions about my past. The cops gave me a lie detector test and said I didn't exactly pass. It's like everything's spinning out of control."

She had trouble following his disjointed thoughts, and as she started to ask a question, Marisol walked over.

"Hey, guys," she said, obviously surprised to see April and her professor in a bar together. "How's it going?"

"Hey, Marisol. I need to talk to you. Back in a sec, Dr. Girard." April led her away from the table. "He called me asking to get together. He says he's about to have a breakdown over Proctor Hall. The house bothered me too, and I'm listening, but I don't think I can help — or if I want to. Look at him — he's a wreck. Something about this really creeps me out."

"Then you know what to do," Marisol said. "Follow your gut, just like you would on a date. Cut him loose. I don't care who he is; you gotta be careful."

She returned to the table and told Julien she understood his concerns. Not only was the house frightening, he had found his student decapitated in the bed and discovered the pumpkin heads. It was enough to make anyone question his sanity.

"I think you should talk to a professional," she said. "Maybe I should too. I don't understand my own feelings about this, and I'm not qualified to give advice to somebody else." She glanced at her watch. 10:15. "I need to go now; I'm sorry."

He said he understood and promised not to talk about Proctor Hall if she would stay long enough to finish their drinks. The conversation would do him good.

With less than half a beer left and sitting in a crowded bar, she stayed. She asked about the projects. "Ours took a turn no one expected. With all the stuff going on, are we still eligible for an A?"

He nodded. "You'll get you're a, April. After losing two team members and going through what you and Marisol have, you deserve it. Cheers to two real troupers." He clinked his bottle with hers and they drank them down. He said he'd pay, thanked her for coming, and went to the bar to settle his tab. She walked out into the cool evening air and entered campus from the back. Her dorm was only three blocks away.

When she missed the mandatory midnight check-in, her floor advisor called campus police. When she hadn't returned by dawn, New Orleans' finest descended on the campus.

CHAPTER THIRTY-TWO

When Landry emerged from the shower, he smelled the aroma of bacon. "Save some for me!" he yelled, and Cate told him to check out the TV.

She clicked on a news story she'd rewound and said, "Get ready for this." The title at the bottom of the screen told it all. *PROFESSOR SOUGHT IN STUDENT'S DISAPPEARANCE.*

"Julien?" he asked, and she nodded.

The newscaster said New Orleans police went to campus around five a.m. on a missing persons report. Several people reported seeing a female student — name withheld — earlier in the evening at a popular off-campus bar. She was in deep conversation with a history professor named Dr. Julien Girard.

Witnesses saw the girl leave Boots Bar around ten. Credit card receipts showed Girard paid the check at the same time and walked out right behind her. Neither had been seen since.

"There is no evidence of foul play," an NOPD spokeswoman said. "We're looking into the relationship between the student and Girard, who's a person of interest. We would like to speak with him. If anyone knows his whereabouts, please call the police."

The news astounded Landry. He'd visited Julien just yesterday afternoon. Was their confrontation connected somehow to this situation? It seemed unlikely, although Landry had learned over the years that life held few coincidences.

Cate said, "Let's consider the facts." Landry had confronted Julien about the people he called his parents, who had a connection to Noah Proctor. Landry had discovered Julien forged the signature on Noah's death certificate, and hours after their heated meeting, he'd met a student in an off-campus bar. Then they both vanished.

At the office, he listened to a voicemail from Marisol asking him to call as soon as possible. She'd left the call at 7:15, around the time he and Cate first heard the story on the news.

Her words came fast. "I saw them, Landry! I was at Boots last night. April took me aside and said he was creeping her out. I watched them both leave, April first and Julien a minute or two later." She'd called the police when she saw the news report, and someone was coming to take her statement.

"I feel terrible I didn't do more," she lamented. "If he abducted her, that is. I can't imagine he'd do something like that, but the world is crazy. She said he seemed different. And he looked terrible. Rumpled clothes, hadn't shaved or put his hair in a ponytail. Something's really wrong, and I hope April is okay."

THE PROCTOR HALL HORROR

Landry said she did the right thing by telling April to heed her instincts, and it seemed the girl had followed Marisol's suggestion. They exchanged cell numbers to stay in touch if something new developed.

He called Shane Young, an NOPD detective with whom he had become friends as they worked together on several paranormal cases. He told the cop about his confrontation with Julien and that he stole the journal to compare the handwriting. It matched perfectly the fake doctor's handwriting on Noah's death certificate.

"Sounds like a desperate man who's not who he seemed. Did he ever give you reason to believe he might harm someone else?"

"No, although he's changed a lot since I met him. He used to be outgoing and happy, but lately he's been depressed and withdrawn. But that's no surprise. Look what he experienced at Proctor Hall. He lay in a bed covered in the blood of his own student — a headless corpse — and he found the jack-o'-lanterns on the mantel. It's enough to make anybody question his sanity, but to me he didn't seem like a kidnapper. Then again, who does?"

Young said, "I'll tell the guys on the case that you called. But I want you to do something for me. Consider that Professor Girard may be nothing like his public persona. We get cases where the perp leads a double life."

"Like a modern-day Jekyll and Hyde?"

"That's what I'm asking you to consider. Thinking outside the box is easy for you, because of the work you do. I don't care what's going on at a plantation in Lafourche Parish or an abandoned house in Lockport. My focus is on a missing college student and the person who either abducted her or knows where she is."

They promised to keep in touch as things developed, and Landry left the office for a stroll around the Quarter. Rarely introspective, today he consider how Shane Young seemed more on target about Dr. Girard than he. Maybe it was the old forest-and-the-trees thing.

Have I been so involved in the Proctor Hall mystery that I'm overlooking everything else? Did I accept everything about Julien at face value, ignoring the real reason he came to Proctor Hall that day? Had the house been new to him, or did he know it like the back of his hand?

Look at it outside the box, Landry.

Instead of an innocent bystander at Michael's decapitation, was Julien the perpetrator? Did he carve the jack-o'-lanterns and arrange them on the mantel?

Did he scrawl the word CRAZY in charcoal on the wall? Is Julien the person the spirit called CRAZY?

Some of those things couldn't have happened in the short timeframe, Landry decided. Julien had been in the bedroom with Michael for only a few minutes. He couldn't decapitate the burly football player without creating a ruckus. They also found no murder weapon. How did he hide it that quickly?

As for the pumpkin heads, he'd bounded down the stairs just moments ahead of the others. He had no time to pull out the pre-carved pumpkins from a hiding place, put them on the mantel, and write the word on the wall.

Despite those facts, Landry believed Julien played a far bigger part in this story. He just hadn't put the pieces together yet. He returned to the office, called Cate, and asked her to set up another lunch with Henri, a man on whom he relied a lot these days. Henri always knew how to find answers to questions that had none.

CHAPTER THIRTY-THREE

The frenzy of lunchtime at Mr. B's Bistro was winding down when Landry and Cate arrived a little after one. They took a window table on the Iberville Street side, placed a wine order, and set aside the menus. Today it would be talk first, lunch second.

He brought Henri current on things and admitted overlooking important signals when focused on a paranormal case. He wondered if they'd all misread Julien Girard's motives — and the man himself.

"It's hard to imagine his being a violent person," Henri admitted. "If it's in his personality, he's learned to hide it well. That said, one never really knows another person's secrets, even those to whom you're closest."

Cate laughed. "We're aware of yours, Henri. It's a glass of perfectly decanted Chateauneuf-du-Pape."

"That's a weakness, not a secret. I'm afraid every waiter in town is aware of that foible. But Dr. Girard's is a different story. None of us knows him well, and as humans often do, we accepted his backstory and his motives at face value.

BILL THOMPSON

Until recently, we had no reason to question anything about the man. Landry, the matter of the forged death certificate is intriguing. And his apparent involvement with April's disappearance is baffling. To realize we were in the company of someone so dangerous alarms me. That's if he was involved, which might not be the case at all."

Landry was certain about his involvement. "I wonder what we can find out about his childhood and his parents. The cops will check his background, and Shane will give me whatever he can, but I wonder if I can find out more."

Cate asked about April. The girl's disappearance worried her very much, and she wondered where he took her and if she could still be alive.

Landry said, "Without knowing his motive, it's impossible to say. April told Marisol that night at the bar he wanted to talk, and we can hope that he abducted her to do just that. Whatever his plans, he'll kill her if someone doesn't find her first. He can't afford to keep her alive after what he's done."

Later that afternoon, Landry accessed birth certificates in the state of Louisiana's records database. He searched for the name Girard in Lafourche Parish and found Joseph and Mary, but not Julien or the brother he mentioned. A statewide search for Julien Girard turned up three, two in their eighties and one in his thirties. No matches there.

He had a crazy idea. What if Julien wasn't who he claimed to be at all? He felt a tingle of excitement as he entered the name Julien *Proctor* in Lafourche Parish. The database churned and spit out Hiram, Susan, Noah and May Ellen — the ill-fated family, three of whom died in the massacre. But no Julien Proctor.

Jack hadn't gotten back with information about the family burials, so he pulled up the Proctor death certificates. The

THE PROCTOR HALL HORROR

same parish medical examiner signed each, and in the space for the place of burial were the words "family plot."

Landry wasn't aware of a cemetery at Proctor Hall, and he buzzed Jack to ask if he'd found anything about a plot there.

"No, and I'm sorry to report I don't have your other answers either. This case has me baffled."

Landry grinned. "That's unlike you. Guess I gave you too much to handle." Jack had a knack for finding things others missed, and it was rare for him to admit defeat.

"The less I discovered, the harder I dug," he continued, "but nothing turned up. Something's strange about all these people. If there's a family plot, nobody I contacted knows where it is. Ben Trimble and his wife, Agnes — the caretakers who took Noah in after his release from the institution — are an enigma too. They were at the house in 1998 when Marguey Slattery disappeared, but by 2018 the two of them had vanished, along with Noah.

"Speaking of Marguey, I found nothing about her either. The only fact we know is that she disappeared. I think because it was sensational, the media called it an abduction when it might have been something else.

"Noah was around then, and everybody already considered him a murderer. Nobody considered alternatives — that Marguey might have run away or drowned in the bayou or been seized by a wild animal or a gator. All I know about her is nothing."

Jack laughed at himself, saying his failure to find answers only created more questions. "My learning so little is unusual in itself. Lots of people disappeared over the years, but now everyone we look for is gone. The bodies of the Proctors are missing. The caretaker and his wife are gone.

BILL THOMPSON

Noah and Marguey Slattery too. What happened to all of them, and is this all part of one gigantic puzzle?"

Landry thanked him for trying and leaned back in his chair to think. What if April's disappearance had something to do with Proctor Hall too? What if it was the most recent unexplained mystery?

CHAPTER THIRTY-FOUR

By daybreak, there was a statewide alert for Julien's silver Toyota Corolla. Every cop in every village in Louisiana, Texas and Mississippi was on the lookout for a fifty-three-year-old white male with a ponytail and a black female aged twenty.

The alert came too late. Around two in the morning outside Lockport, the Corolla rolled down an embankment and slipped into Bayou Lafourche. It was plenty deep here — Julien knew that from the countless hours he'd spent as a boy fishing off this same bank.

As the car sank, he had a moment of regret. He liked that car, and it was just two years old and not yet paid off. But then he chuckled. From this point forward, like other things that had mattered once, the car and its monthly payments meant nothing now.

In one fleeting moment last night, Julien had crossed a point of no return. He left behind his facade — the well-crafted persona of a university professor. He took a bold step, made a choice, and traded one life for another.

BILL THOMPSON

For however many years or days or hours he had left, he would belong to the shadow world that had always inhabited his psyche. Before, he would visit it occasionally to experience its pleasures, but he always returned to the other life. Until now.

He walked a mile down the road, gratified that no cars passed him at this late hour. Inside a rickety old barn, he pulled back a tarp to uncover the Vespa he'd hidden earlier, headed west until he came to a familiar turnoff into a cane field, and drove to the cabin.

When he entered, he heard moans from the bedroom. She was just now waking up. The stuff he'd put in her beer knocked her out longer than he expected.

Her eyes displayed terror as she struggled against the plastic ties that secured her hands and feet. In this remote place he felt safe removing the gag from her mouth. She took deep, gasping breaths and tried to sit up. Julien observed every move with fascination. He'd never done something like this before, and he was interested to see how a person in such a situation reacted.

"You'll never get away with this!"

He smiled, brought over a chair, and sat in front of her. "Get away with what, April? What's my goal? Why did I bring you here? You don't know what I'm after, so perhaps I already have gotten away with it."

"Kidnappers get the death penalty, you bastard. You put something in my beer when I walked away to talk to Marisol. They'll find you. The cops must be combing the area right now."

"They wouldn't be good at their jobs if they weren't," he replied. "Soon there will be roadblocks and house-to-house searches and everything in between. I can only imagine. If I had a television or my cell phone, I could follow the news. But now I have no use for either of those things. And we're far, far away from anywhere they'll be looking."

"Give me some water."

"Have you forgotten your manners? Even in a situation like ours, it's only civil to be polite. Now ask me again."

"Please. Please give me some water. I'm thirsty."

He brought a bottle from the cooler, opened it, and held it to her lips as she drank. She looked into his eyes — this wasn't the professor she'd had a beer with last night. His mannerisms, his inflections, and even his face had changed. This was someone else — a man with a purpose, the type of man she had hoped never to meet.

"What are you going to do to me?"

Julien smiled. "Don't be afraid. It will only tax your strength. I apologize for binding your hands and feet, but I think we both agree it's for the best. We don't want them to find you until I'm ready."

"Ready for what?"

"Ready to show our friend Mr. Drake the Proctor Hall horror. He must be beside himself with questions that have no answers. I'll give him everything he needs, and you will be an important part of that revelation."

"I...I don't understand."

"But you will, I promise. Why don't you try to rest now? I have things to do. I'll be away for a while, but I'll bring you something to eat when I return."

BILL THOMPSON

As he knelt to put the cover over her mouth, she tried to bite his hand. He slapped her hard and then apologized. "I'm sorry, April. I don't want to hurt you, and if you cooperate with me, the only hurting will be at the end."

At the end? His words echoed in the room as she fought to breathe through her nose.

April understood. It would be the end of her twenty years on Earth.

CHAPTER THIRTY-FIVE

In the two days since April's abduction, lawmen had combed the area for the girl and the professor. They spent untold man-hours searching Proctor Hall, the plantation's outbuildings, and the house in Lockport.

Officers tore apart April's dorm room and, as expected, they found nothing helpful. They went to Julien's house — the domicile of a messy bachelor, with clothes, books and papers carelessly tossed about. Investigators who found his computer noted the hard drive was missing. Although not proof, it was a sign that Julien had planned his disappearance.

While the cops looked for the missing persons, Landry, Cate, Henri and Jack sat in a cozy little bar called Patrick's on Bienville Street.

"We already agreed to have another seance," Landry said. "It has to happen as soon as possible. We may already be too late. Nothing else about Proctor Hall matters except April."

Cate said, "So you think she's in the house? How? The cops have been over every square inch of it. Isn't another seance there just a waste of time?"

Landry's theory was that Julien took April somewhere else. They needed to find the motive for why he took her. Whatever his connection to Proctor Hall, it played a part in the kidnapping. One thing was certain — Julien was no ordinary university professor, and the entities in the house might give them clues to help find her.

"We're out of time. I want to do the seance tomorrow. Cate, see if your dad wants to come back over. I'll get Phil to check out a van and meet us at Cafe du Monde at eight."

Doc couldn't come; he'd spent too much time away from his busy practice, and Jack was busy too. The others grabbed coffee and beignets before piling into the van for the trip back to Lafourche Parish.

As they neared Thibodaux, Landry remembered he'd intended to buy a Ouija board. In the hubbub yesterday afternoon, it had slipped his mind.

"Friends in the paranormal business sometimes come in handy." Henri laughed, patting his backpack. "I brought one just in case." The pack was all Henri had this time; since they were short on time, he'd left his complicated gear at the office.

Landry, Cate and Henri unloaded the table and chairs and carried them into the sitting room while Phil set up his camera. They sat at the table and rested their fingers on the pointer.

Landry began with, "Is anybody home?" and Cate rolled her eyes.

THE PROCTOR HALL HORROR

"God, Landry. You're not stopping by somebody's house for tea. Henri, why don't you be the communicator? At least you know something about it."

After ten minutes of unsuccessful attempts, they decided they should have hired a medium. The DIY method just wasn't working. Henri reached for the planchette to pack it away, and the moment his fingers touched it, the pointer moved.

D-A-N-G-E-R.

"Danger for whom?" Henri whispered, and the planchette spelled *F-R-I-E-N-D*.

"We think our friend April is in danger. Are you talking about her?"

YES

"Where is she?"

NOT HERE

"Does a man have her?"

YES DANGER

"We must save her. Do you know where she is?"

SHE WANTS APRIL

"Who? You said a man has her. That's Julien, right?"

SHE WANTS APRIL DANGER

"Who is she?"

SHE IS BAD

Landry whispered, "Find out who the spirit is talking about."

Even though no one asked a question, the pointer moved.

NOAH

"Is Noah going to hurt April?"

SHE IS BAD

Next he asked the question that would have been his first of the day if things hadn't started off by veering in a different direction.

"Who are you?"

ME

"Same person," Cate murmured. "May Ellen Proctor."

The planchette shot across the board so rapidly that they couldn't keep their fingers on it. This time they weren't driving the pointer. Something else was, and the letters came flying.

L-E-A-V-E-T-H-I-S-H-O-U-S-E

LEAVE THIS HOUSE, said the Ouija board not once, but three times.

"I don't think we're talking to May Ellen anymore," Henri observed, putting his fingers back on the pointer.

He asked, "Tell me who you are."

LEAVE OR DIE

CHAPTER THIRTY-SIX

Henri said, "Perhaps we *should* leave," but Landry had a hunch and wanted a turn.

He put fingertips to the planchette and said, "I'm sorry to disturb you, Agnes, but our friend is in danger. You are Agnes Trimble, correct?"

LEAVE NOW

"We won't leave without our friend April. Where is she?"

A dozen books flew from a shelf next to the fireplace and crashed onto the floor.

"She's pissed," Cate cried. "Henri, this is getting out of hand."

DANGER

"Landry, stop it! We have to go!"

Landry shouted, "You know where Julien Girard is. I command you to tell me now!"

In seconds a cloud of thick smoke issued from the fireplace, engulfing them in an inky blackness so thick Landry couldn't see the Ouija board that was mere inches from his face, much less the others in the room.

"Keep your fingers on the pointer!" Henri yelled. "This is a power play. Don't let her win!"

The mist boiled around Landry as he pressed down hard with his fingertips. The planchette moved around the board, but in the dark no one could tell which letters it stopped on.

Henri moved his fingers around the board until he found the pointer. He touched it and said, "Leave us alone! We are not here to disturb you. We want Julien and April. Where are they?"

As quickly as it formed, the cloud sucked back into the fireplace in an enormous swirl of darkness. The room was as before, and the planchette moved.

G-O-N-E

"Where did they go? Are they on this property?"

GOODBYE

"Wait! Answer me!"

The board became quiet. The spirit had departed.

It frustrated Landry that the seance revealed almost nothing new. The spirit called a woman bad. Was she referring to Agnes Trimble, the caretaker's wife who tossed the books out of the shelf. Everything else made no sense. The word GONE, for instance. Was that a reference to April or to someone else?

THE PROCTOR HALL HORROR

As they drove back, Landry said he wanted one last shot at Proctor Hall. He would drop the others in town, return to the house, and survey it from a safe distance for a few hours, in case something happened.

If Proctor Hall didn't hold the answers they needed, at least it had played a part in everything they witnessed. Julien's connection to the house was a mystery. They knew one thing — with every passing minute, April might be in more danger. She might already be dead, but until they had proof, Landry would keep trying to find her.

The others liked the stakeout idea, but when Landry said he'd do it solo, Henri and Cate balked. "Take someone with you," they urged, and Phil volunteered. But Landry said he planned to observe, not engage. He'd stay out of sight and keep quiet. The fewer people, the better. He insisted on doing this one alone.

A half hour before sunset, Landry pulled his Jeep off the highway and parked it in an oak grove. He carried a backpack down the rutted lane and selected a spot in the trees a hundred yards from the house, with a good view of it and the road. As stars appeared in the cloudless sky, he set up a folding chair and a small camp table, popped a beer, and adjusted the light on his phone screen to low. Then he settled back to wait.

He knew this might be another bust, but he had run out of ideas. After three hours, a check-in text to Cate, and a thousand games of Solitaire, he heard a faint noise.

Off in the distance came the sound of an engine — a small one. At first it came from the highway, but then it was louder, and soon a Vespa scooter emerged from the lane. The driver — a person in dark clothing — parked by the house. He got off and removed his helmet. In the pale moonlight, Landry noticed the long black ponytail. The quarry had come, as Landry hoped. Julien Girard had arrived.

As Julien flipped on a flashlight, unlocked the door and entered, Landry ran across the yard to the nearest window and looked through it. The beam from Julien's light revealed his whereabouts — first the music room and then down the hall to the kitchen. Then without warning he appeared in the room Landry was looking into. Just five feet away, he played the beam of light across the window seconds after Landry ducked.

When Julien went upstairs, Landry crossed the porch, eased open the door, and crept inside. He heard footsteps and a muffled conversation.

Was someone else in the house? The place had been quiet for as long as he'd been watching, but that meant nothing. He crept up a few stairs, paused, and listened to two voices. One was Julien's, and the other, a raspy, unfamiliar one, sounded female. They were arguing.

Julien said, "When will this stop? You ruined my career, and for what?"

A harsh laugh. "You blame me? I didn't tell you to take the girl. Your career means nothing to me. Family, history, legacy — those are the only things that matter. Continuing to show everyone Noah Proctor is a cold-blooded killer is what's important to me."

A long, deep sigh like the lowest notes of an instrument echoed throughout the house. Landry noticed chilly air encircling him, and he realized he stood on the fourth riser — the one where Noah sat after his family died. A sensation of profound sadness swept through his mind.

Julien said, "But he's not a killer, Mother. It's been years — decades. Why allow the sore to fester? Why keep this

THE PROCTOR HALL HORROR

bizarre charade alive? You've accomplished the goal. Everyone blames Noah, even to this day. Why can't you let it go?"

"Are we remorseful tonight? That's not a good look for you. Cheer up, Julien. You've experienced the euphoria of taking a life. What an amazing feeling! Soon you'll do it again — the girl is yours to do with as you wish. And Noah too. When I'm ready, I'll let you do the honors."

"I'm not you, Mother. I felt the euphoria, yes, but you're different. You're…insane and you know it. The other day you killed my student, Michael. There was no call for that, and I might have gone to prison for it. I gave up the life I had for you. I'll deal with the girl, but then I'm finished. Noah's your problem. You should have eliminated him years ago, but you delighted in keeping him around. Your lunacy is your issue, and I refuse to let you make it mine."

The old house creaked and the windowpanes rattled as a strong breeze arose from nowhere. A mournful sound emanated from downstairs, rising in intensity until it was a screeching wail. Landry sensed a presence in the hallway next to him, but he saw nothing.

"Look at what you've done!" Julien screamed. "You've stirred them up."

A dark thing appeared in the hallway — a wraith wearing black that floated toward him. The thing raised its arm, and a bony finger pointed at him. He drew back in alarm. It swept closer and now Landry realized it was pointing not at him, but to the stairway above.

He looked up and saw an old woman grinning as she descended the stairs. She had something in her hand — something that she swung through the air toward Landry's head. It connected solidly and there was nothing.

CHAPTER THIRTY-SEVEN

After worrying during Landry's harrowing adventures, he and Cate had established an emergency plan. If he was away on a paranormal assignment by himself, he would communicate every three hours. No call meant something was wrong.

Tonight she got a text at eight, and she lay in bed waiting for another. At eleven fifteen she left Landry a message and called Harry Kanter. The cop understood her concern, but he told her it was too early for him to become involved. He had to wait twenty-four hours from the last communication before filing a missing persons report.

"He texted you at eight, so it'll be tomorrow night before we can investigate. You might try calling the sheriff's office in Thibodaux. Even if they have a waiting period like ours, they're local. Their guys patrol all over the parish. If a car's in the vicinity, they might send an officer to Proctor Hall to check things out."

She had no connections in the sheriff's department, so she called the dispatcher and explained her concern. The woman recited protocol about domestic disputes, which pissed Cate off.

"This is no domestic dispute, lady," she fired back. "Do you know who Landry Drake is?"

"The ghost hunter? Sure. Who doesn't?"

"Okay. He's my…uh, colleague, and he's the one missing at Proctor Hall. He checked in with me at eight and should have again at eleven. It's a huge red flag when he misses a check-in. It's a signal something's wrong."

The dispatcher's attitude changed in an instant. A celebrity disappearing in a sparsely populated rural parish would mean lots of publicity. If the sheriff ignored Landry Drake's going missing in his parish, it might come down on everybody, especially her.

"Hold on a moment," she said. Cate listened as she got on the radio.

"One-four, this is base. What's your twenty?"

"I'm on 308 coming into Larose. What's up?"

"Possible 10-57 at Proctor Hall. Can you stop by and look around?"

"10-4. Should be there in thirty-forty minutes unless you want me to light 'er up and do it quicker."

"No. Just check it out and radio me when you're done."

Cate gave the dispatcher her cell number and the combination to the gate padlock at Proctor Hall. The woman said she'd call as soon as she knew something.

THE PROCTOR HALL HORROR

Cate was waiting in the living room with the phone in her hand when the return call came at 12:26 a.m. The deputy reported the house was dark, there were no cars around the house, and he saw no sign of activity.

She had two options. One was Henri, who would be asleep at this late hour, but he would do anything to help Landry. She hated to get him up when this might be as simple as a poor cellular connection.

Instead, she called Phil. If he thought Landry was in trouble, he'd go, but tonight he didn't answer. She left a message explaining what had happened and that she was going to Proctor Hall to find him. As terrifying as it was, she had to handle this one alone.

She arrived around two and found everything dark and still. She circled the house, calling Landry's name, and ended up back at the car. Without a plan, she held the key for a long time and wondered what Landry would do. That foolish thought made her smile. He'd barge in like a bull, safety be damned, and get himself into a predicament. But wouldn't she be doing the same thing if she went through that door?

She received her answer in an unexpected and chilling way. Sitting in her car and wondering what to do, she saw a light inside. It flickered like a candle, drifted across an upstairs window, and disappeared.

Oh God, somebody's in the house! If it's not Landry, then who's here?

Terrified to do what she knew she must, Cate put the key in the lock, took a deep breath, and stepped over the threshold into the shadows.

Please don't let Noah be sitting on the stairs.

Nothing moved, and the only sounds were the creaks and rattles that a drafty old house made. Cate tiptoed up the stairs far enough to see the hallway. No one was there, and all four bedroom doors were open. Through the windows, moonbeams played on the walls and floors, creating an undulating shimmer of ghostly shapes.

"Who's...is anybody here? Landry, can you hear me?" Her voice cracked as she stammered the words. If someone was in here, they now knew she was too.

"May Ellen, help me. Please help me find Landry."

"I can give you answers."

The whispered words echoed in the empty hallway. They might have come from anywhere.

"May Ellen?"

There was a low, guttural laugh — long and drawn out like the one in the seance. "I'm something that inhabits your nightmares. Do you want your man back enough to face me?"

"Where are you?"

"Maybe inside your head. Maybe just up the stairs. Maybe right behind you."

Cate jerked backwards, missed the step, and tumbled down, banging her knee against the railing as she fell. As she sat up and tested her legs, she looked up the staircase.

At the top stood a figure dressed in black. Something in its hand gleamed in the moonlight. Something metallic.

A hatchet.

THE PROCTOR HALL HORROR

She screamed and screamed as the ghostly entity descended the stairs one slow step at a time.

A wave of helplessness and fear she'd never experienced coursed through her body. She trembled and cried for help as the figure moved closer.

The last thing Cate recalled was the room spinning, the thing lifting its draped arms, and a merciful nothingness as her consciousness faded.

CHAPTER THIRTY-EIGHT

Regaining consciousness in utter darkness, Landry felt a throbbing in his right temple that outshone any headache known to man. He touched the place carefully; it would hurt like hell, but it was superficial.

He smelled a powerful, musty odor — the airless, moldy scent of an ancient place. He lay on a dirt floor, and when he put out his hands, he felt a damp earthen wall. As he stood, he banged against a low ceiling and fell to the ground, more pain shooting through his already throbbing head.

He moved around the room to determine its size. It was empty except at the far end, where something solid connected with his foot. Just then he realized his phone was in his pocket, and tried to call Cate, but there was no signal. He flipped on the flashlight and found he was in a ten-foot-square room with dirt walls and floor. The ceiling consisted of wood joists that might be the floor of a room above.

The thing he bumped into was a large wooden box longer than it was wide and three feet high. It looked like a coffin, and then a sound came from inside — a series of knocks.

Someone's in there! "April! April, I'm here to help you!" The sound stopped, and he examined the top, seeing three large hinges on one side and an old metal hasp with a four-inch nail holding it shut. He tugged on the nail until it came out, unhooked the hasp, and raised the lid.

A person lay inside. Not April, but a man of indeterminate age whose pasty-white complexion hadn't seen sunlight for a long time. Matted, dirty gray hair hung in strings down to his shoulders. When he sat up and put his hands on the sides of the box, Landry noticed his long grimy fingernails.

"Who are you?" he asked, but the man stared at him and gave no response.

With some difficulty he rose to his feet, and Landry noticed a chain around his ankles and tethered to a bolt in the floor. The bottom of the box was damp; a little water had seeped in from recent rains, and the poor guy had been forced to lie in it. The man turned away and unashamedly urinated on the floor beside the box.

Landry asked, "What is this place? Where are we?"

The man looked at him but didn't respond.

He's not deaf, so why won't he answer?

Then he understood. He'd found Noah, the man who never spoke. Perhaps mute, perhaps autistic — no one was certain which — people claimed he hadn't spoken a word since birth. Here lay an accused mass murderer who spent half his life in an asylum.

"Noah, my name is Landry. If you'll let me, I'll help you."

Landry tugged on the chain, finding it secure and impossible to unhook without tools. A few minutes later

THE PROCTOR HALL HORROR

there came a scraping noise from somewhere above, and Noah reclined in the box.

Light filtered in as someone opened a trapdoor in the ceiling. Landry snapped off his phone and moved to a corner. Someone lowered a crude wooden ladder into the room. He saw shoes, and then legs, and he struck.

He body-slammed the ladder, knocking the person to the ground. He landed a hard kick to the torso, and there came a grunt. A familiar voice cried, "Dammit, Landry, stop! You're killing me!"

He switched on the flashlight. "Phil! What are you doing here?"

"I was trying to save your ass until you assaulted me. Damn, man, you kicked the hell out of me. I think my ribs are broken."

"Sorry. I never expected you to climb down that ladder. Speaking of which, where are we?"

"In a hidden room below the old sugar mill. If I hadn't followed the people who brought you here, I'd never have seen it. There's old equipment lying around everywhere, and the entrance to this vault is under some of it."

Phil noticed the man lying in the box. "Who the hell is that?"

"Noah Proctor, I think. He doesn't talk. Let's get out of here while we can."

"Too late!" The words came through the open trapdoor as they ran toward the ladder. And it was true — they really were too late. The door slammed shut and there was a dragging noise.

BILL THOMPSON

"He's moving junk back over the door to hide it," Phil said.

"Did you recognize the voice?"

"Yeah. It's the professor we saw earlier."

Landry nodded and asked Phil to help him search for an exit. As Noah watched impassively, they examined the seams where the earthen walls intersected with the joists above. They found nothing helpful there or in the ceiling. They found loose boards, but with junk and equipment stacked on them, they wouldn't budge.

They turned off their lights to conserve power, and Landry asked again how Phil had ended up at Proctor Hall. "You followed me, didn't you?"

"No, I beat you here. I just hid and waited until you came creeping down the lane. You made me jealous when you played games on your phone. I had to sit behind you in the woods and be quiet the whole time. When Julien Girard came on his scooter, you peeked through the window and went inside. I hid in the bushes next to the porch and was about to come looking for you when the door opened.

"I thought you'd died when I saw two people come out, one holding your shoulders and the other your feet. With no weapon and up against two of them, I stayed put for a minute. I was damn glad when the woman dropped your legs and you groaned."

"The *woman*? One of my attackers was a woman? Might it have been April?"

"No way. She had long hair, and she was old and bent like she had arthritis. I couldn't see a face, but I definitely heard a woman's voice. Croaky, like a frog's, but female."

"What did she say?"

THE PROCTOR HALL HORROR

"She said she couldn't carry you that far, and the professor hoisted you up on his shoulders in a fireman's carry. When he went off into the woods with you on his back, I was surprised at his strength. I followed him along a trail he knew well. Even when the trees blocked the moonlight and it was pitch black, he kept moving.

"He brought you here. It's a ruined brick building with only four walls standing. The roof collapsed a long time ago, and like I said, there are rusted metal machines and tools everywhere. Girard knew exactly where to go. He pushed aside an old wagon, opened the trapdoor, dumped you inside, and left. I waited a few minutes before I snuck down the ladder and you tried to kill me."

"I guess I'm lucky you disobeyed my order and came anyway. Thanks for caring enough to follow me."

"Somebody has to keep you out of trouble, boss. Speaking of trouble, I didn't do that great a rescue job. What do we do now?"

"We hope one of them comes back. I want to find out who the woman is."

"Think maybe before she kills us, she'll introduce herself?"

Landry snorted a reply and settled back to wait.

CHAPTER THIRTY-NINE

Phil asked Landry how he was certain the other person in their prison was Noah Proctor.

"Stands to reason. The age is about right and he doesn't speak. I suppose he might be someone else, but I'll bet I'm right." He turned on the light and walked to the box that held the man.

"Noah, we want to help you, but we have to get away first. Any idea how we can get out of here?"

He stared into Landry's eyes without expression or words, watching as Landry and Phil searched every square inch of the place. At last they gave up, sat down, came up with a plan, and waited.

Someone walked across the floor above them, and they moved into position. Landry had the ladder; if they got the opportunity, one of them would scramble up and overpower whoever was there. There was the sliding sound and the trapdoor opened.

"Hello, gentlemen. I hope everything's satisfactory."

"Julien, what the hell are you doing?" Landry said. "You kidnapped April and now you're just making everything worse for yourself. You won't get away with this."

"I'm at the point I don't *want* to get away with it. Have you considered that? Perhaps I'm ready to give up the I that has been my life."

"There are people out there who can help you. I promise —"

"Don't promise what you can't deliver," said a voice from above. It was the woman Landry had heard Julien arguing with at Proctor Hall — the one he'd called mother.

"You're going to kill them, right?" she said to Julien.

"Mother, stop it. For once, we're doing things my way. I don't need April any more now that we have Landry Drake. She was uncovering too many secrets, but she's weak. Now we have the person I most wanted, the ghost hunter himself. I can't wait to tell him everything about Proctor Hall. Before he dies, of course."

"No!" the woman screamed. "You cannot tell our secrets. I forbid it. You'll ruin everything. Kill the girl like you promised. Then we can kill these two as well."

"Yes, yes, I will. First things first. She's not going anywhere. I have to think about these two now. I've enticed my students to explore Proctor Hall every semester, but I've kept the truths hidden. I'm bursting to tell someone. Landry! I have to tell him about the Proctor Hall horror. The *real* horror. That would be you, Mother."

As the argument intensified, Landry moved the ladder to the hole in the ceiling. The captors seemed to have forgotten about them, and it might be their only chance to

THE PROCTOR HALL HORROR

escape. He placed the ladder and prepared to spring up the rungs, when the woman let out a screeching yell. A second later the hole turned dark, and something large fell onto Landry.

Landry crawled from under his bulk as the old woman muttered, "Can't even depend on family these days," and slammed the trapdoor. She moved the debris back over it and walked away.

"Capturing you wasn't my idea," Julien said as they sat on the ground, their only light coming from Phil's phone screen.

"You expect me to believe that? I listened to what you said. You kidnapped April and you're going to kill her. I can't wait to testify against you. The death penalty's too good for you. At least you'll burn in hell for eternity."

"This isn't what it seems."

"Bullshit. How many people are you holding captive? There are at least four — the three of us and April. Where's Andy Arnaud? Did you kill him, or is he in another dungeon like this one? And this guy you keep in a box with the lid locked. What's that about? He's Noah Proctor, I'm sure. Why is he your captive too?"

"It's Mother. It's all her fault."

Phil had had enough. He flew across the room and hit Julien squarely in the chest. He pummeled the man with his fists until Landry pulled him off.

"You lying bastard," Phil said as he stood. "You're a damned piece of shit!"

BILL THOMPSON

Julien said, "I'll tell you everything. It's too late now. The best we can hope is she never comes back and we starve to death. She's killed so many people..."

Landry turned on his phone's recorder. If they died, someone would find the bodies and learn what had happened. "Where's April?"

"She's safe. When I get out of here — if I do — I'll set her free. I never intended to kill her. I took her for her own good. Mother wanted her to die because she was a psychic. She was learning too much. Now that Mother has you, I can let April go."

Landry couldn't believe anything the man said, but he was in no position to bargain or argue with him. Instead, he wanted to keep Julien talking. "Who the hell are you? You're no college professor, that's for sure. Who is this serial killer mother of yours? Is it Mary Girard?"

"No. The Girards raised me from birth," he said. "My real mother refused to deal with a child. It wasn't her fault; she was mentally ill. It was really far more than mental illness. She was a homicidal maniac. Nobody suspected anything because when it got bad, my father locked her up in a cage. We saw it that day Henri took us on the house tour. I didn't reveal it then, but I should have directed the tour through Proctor Hall that day. Hell, I was born there, although my parents gave me to the Girards that same day."

"I don't get it. The house belonged to the Proctors. You said earlier you aren't a Proctor. Was that a lie?"

"No. The Proctor Hall Massacre happened in 1963, four years before I was born. Another family occupied the house by then. I'm not a Proctor. I'm a Trimble. I'm Ben and Agnes Trimble's only child."

CHAPTER FORTY

Landry said, "You're the child of the caretaker and his wife. Everyone thinks they moved away and took Noah with them." He pointed to the box. "Noah's right there, so they never left at all."

Julien said it wasn't as simple as that. "Agnes — my birth mother — has been mentally ill her whole life. From what I've learned, she seemed normal when Ben married her, but things spiraled out of control over the years. He built that cage and locked her up at night. He freed her during the daytime, thinking it safe because they had no visitors. The supervisor, Mike, stopped by occasionally, but no one else came. Even then, Ben kept a close eye on her. She was unpredictable and capable of horrific things.

"At around eleven I learned the Girards weren't my birth parents. To most kids, it would have been a shock, but I felt grateful. As a child, we rarely visited Proctor Hall. Each time we did, Agnes screamed and ranted from somewhere upstairs. My stepmom called her crazy and refused to allow me to see her. That's when I learned her husband locked her in a cage."

"That must have been a surprise."

"Not as much as it would seem. Things at the house were always bizarre. Every time we visited Proctor Hall and my stepmom went upstairs, they got into some big argument that ended in a screaming match."

Landry interrupted. "If she was insane, why did the Girards continue visiting her?"

"Family. Mary Girard was my aunt — Agnes Trimble's sister. We just lived down the road in Lockhart, and my stepmother felt obligated. I was fifteen the last time we visited as a family. That's when my life changed forever. From that day on, I learned to hide my family's and my insanity behind a I."

"What happened?"

"Ben didn't secure the lock, and his wife got out. She snuck down the stairs and found us all in the music room. When she heard her brother-in-law, Joseph, ask about why she had to be in the cage, something snapped. She flew into the room, jumped on Joseph, and clawed his eyeballs out. Within seconds it got worse. She snatched a pair of scissors from a table and stabbed him to death.

"That day I saw the ghosts for the first time. The moment my mother killed her brother-in-law, a groan echoed through the house — more of a piercing sound than a noise. It entered my brain like a needle. Three shadows rose from the floor and encircled Agnes within seconds. Formless at first, they developed into phantoms with human forms — a girl, a man and a woman. The Proctors.

"When they first appeared, Agnes had a crazy grin on her face, but we all watched them push closer and closer, tightening their grip around her, and she uttered a hellish cry of terror that still invades my dreams at night. When she fell to the floor, they disappeared. The entire episode took maybe ten seconds, but it dramatically affected my mother. She whimpered and became submissive, allowing Ben to drag her up to the cage.

"I was only a teenager, but when I watched my mother kill the man who raised me, I was exhilarated, not disgusted." He paused and chuckled. "I can't imagine what you two are thinking right now. What a demented individual this man is. How deranged and sadistic he must be."

Landry and Phil said nothing.

Julien continued, "I realized that the madness was genetic. I worried that I would become like her. My stepmother, Mary, was crazy too. Her sister murdered Mary's husband before her eyes, but instead of being repulsed, she seemed fascinated. It ran in her genes, just like in mine."

"My God," Phil said. "No wonder you're..." He stopped short of finishing.

"Go ahead — say it. Crazy? Demented? A murderer in my own right? They all apply. I'm just like my mother. Until now, I hid it better. In one way it's sad, but in another, confession is cathartic."

Astounded at the man's calm description of the horrors, Landry wondered if Julien could ever be rehabilitated. It was moot if they died in this chamber, but he still wanted answers. He asked what Noah did while Agnes killed her brother-in-law.

"I guess he sat on the stairs. He was so quiet, nobody ever paid any attention to him. Agnes fed him three times a day and made him go to bed and get up, but other than that, he just sat there."

Julien looked across the room at the pale man sitting in the box. "Noah, tell them how it affected you when Agnes killed that man," he taunted. "Don't want to talk right now? That's fine. I'll tell them what you did that day. Noah sat on the fourth stair on the stairway. He could hear everything, but he didn't make a move to help. I often wonder what's inside that mind of his. Does he process like we do? What went on inside his mind the night his entire family died? Did he get a rush like I get?"

Landry glanced at Phil. *Wacko,* he communicated with a roll of his eyes.

He asked what happened to Joseph's body.

"Ben said nobody else needed to know about this. It was a family matter, and he'd take care of the problem. I lived with Mary Girard in Lockport for three more years, and she never even asked what happened to the body. But after that day we never went back to Proctor Hall."

"Didn't people in town wonder what happened to your stepfather?"

"We were loners. People may have asked — I don't remember — but Mary would have told them to mind their own affairs."

Landry pushed harder. "You said you're as maniacal as your mother. What do you mean by that?"

"When I was eighteen and at the house with my stepmother, she did something or said something that set me off. It's odd that I can't remember what it was. Something clicked in my head — something palpable. I felt a switch turn on, and negative energy flowed through my entire being.

THE PROCTOR HALL HORROR

"I turned on her, grabbed a frying pan, and beat her to death with it. Once it was dark, I dragged her body to the bayou and tossed it in. The water began churning and splashing, and I knew the gators had found her. That was that. I went back into the house and finished my supper.

"The feeling I experienced was a bizarre thing hidden inside me since birth, I suppose. It felt good to let it out, although I knew how powerful and dangerous it was. If I were to live any semblance of a normal life, it must stay hidden deep in my psyche."

The words came from a man with no soul. Others might call his actions reprehensible, but from then on Julien didn't care. He wasn't like the others. His mind was infested with maggots — not literally, but his DNA, or brain cells, or something, were missing the ingredient that kept humans on a moral track.

Landry's own mother always said the test of a man was what he would do in a situation if nobody would find out. Such a test would be useless for Julien Girard. He had no sense of guilt or accountability for his actions.

"Will your mother come back and kill us?" Phil asked, and the answer was chilling.

"Us? I doubt that. You, absolutely. She intends to kill both of you. Probably Noah too, since she's delayed doing that for so many years. She's old and tired. I can't see her caring for him any longer."

"Did she keep him alive because he's a maniac like her?"

Puzzled, Julien said, "I'm not sure what you mean."

"He's a homicidal killer. He decapitated his entire family."

Julien chuckled. "Noah? He wouldn't hurt a fly. Noah didn't kill his family — he would never have done that. They loved each other. Family was all he had, and they cared for him every minute of his life."

"So what are you saying?"

The answer never came. There were footsteps above, and then something slid across the floor. The trapdoor opened and a shaft of light pierced the darkness. Agnes Trimble shouted down, "Son, have you killed them yet?"

"Let me out, Mother," Julien said. "We'll leave them down here to die. No one will ever find them."

Phil grabbed Julien, but the man whispered, "Play along. I won't lock the trapdoor and I won't block it. You'll be able to escape."

Landry nodded — he didn't trust Julien, but they had no alternatives. He doubted Agnes even cared if they killed her son.

Julien climbed the ladder and closed the door. Landry and Phil were in the dark once again, listening to faint words they couldn't understand. Then came another sound — the familiar noise of something heavy being dragged across the floor above them.

"Bastard lied to us!" Phil exclaimed, but Landry held a finger to his lips and waited. After two minutes passed, then three, he went to the ladder, climbed up and pushed.

The door flipped up and fell back, wide open. Julien had kept his word.

CHAPTER FORTY-ONE

They crept up into the old mill, regretting having to leave Noah behind. They would return with tools to free him, but first they had to get away from the plantation. Landry's phone dinged to life, and he saw a message from Cate. She'd also left Phil a voicemail, but their priority was to get away from the mill and out of danger.

Since Phil knew what direction the mill was from the house, he also had a good idea where the highway was. Using the phone's compass, they walked through the tall stalks of cane for twenty minutes until they found the highway.

He called but reached Cate's voicemail. He hadn't checked in for sixteen hours and knew she'd be worried. Why would she not have answered? He learned the answer seconds later when Phil played Cate's frantic voicemail. She hadn't gotten a call from Landry and was driving to Proctor Hall to look for him.

"Oh God," Landry cried. "She came to the house!"

BILL THOMPSON

He called Lieutenant Kanter's cell phone, and the cop answered at once.

"Landry! Where are you? Are you okay?"

"Yes. I'm on Highway 308 near Proctor Hall. Cate may be in trouble. How soon can you get here?"

"I'm at the house. Cate called me last night worried about you, and I brought two guys with me to check things out."

Landry arrived at where he'd hidden his Jeep and said, "Thank God you're here. Wait for me. I'll be there in five minutes."

His heart dropped as he saw Cate's car parked next to Kanter's black-and-white at Proctor Hall. He and Phil ran to the porch, where the cops waited. "They kidnapped Phil and me, and we escaped," he blurted, "but Cate came up here last night. That's her car, which means she's here somewhere. We have to find her!"

Kanter drew his weapon, rapped on the door and shouted, "Police! Open up!" Five seconds later he gave a sign to another officer, who kicked the door in. With weapons drawn, the cops rushed inside and moved throughout the house. They cleared the rooms, and Kanter allowed Landry and Phil inside.

"Cate! Cate, are you here? It's me! Where are you?"

From the barred cage upstairs, Cate listened to his shouts. She tried to answer, but the tape over her mouth turned her words into muffled moans. She had heard the officers talking in the hallway, and tried to kick at the bars, but the tape securing her body made it impossible. She heard them going back downstairs and cried.

THE PROCTOR HALL HORROR

Landry told them about Noah Proctor chained in a subterranean room at the old mill. Cate might be imprisoned somewhere near there, and they filed out to the porch to go search for her. Landry was last, and as he stepped through the door, there was a noise from inside — something faint and indistinct, but definitely a sound.

"Everybody, come back in the house and listen!"

There it was again — a knocking sound. Barely perceptible, but a real sound.

"Cate! Cate, knock again!"

Knock, knock, knock. From upstairs.

"Come on!" he yelled, bounding up the stairs. "We didn't check the cage!"

It took the cops two minutes with a bolt cutter to break the chain that held the gate shut. Landry and Phil picked Cate up and carried her into the hall. When he removed the tape from her mouth, she gasped deep breaths of air.

Kanter removed her body tape with a knife. "Good thing you knocked," he commented, and she said that was her last-ditch effort. She'd bumped her heels on the floor just hard enough to make a sound.

He asked who abducted her, and she said there was a phantom on the stairway, wielding a hatchet. When it approached, she blacked out.

Landry helped her downstairs and onto the porch. He said, "Let's get you out of here. I'm taking you home. Phil, show them where Noah is and keep in touch with developments. Lieutenant, thank God you were concerned enough to show up."

BILL THOMPSON

As they drove away, Phil led the officers through rows of cane. "To me, Proctor Hall isn't ever what it seems," he said. "We overheard Agnes and Julien talking about secrets. It pissed her off that he wanted to tell Landry, and she threw him down into the room where we were."

The officer had his pistol in hand when he descended the ladder and found Noah sitting in the wooden coffin. One cop had the bolt cutter, and they made quick work of the chain. Noah seemed confused when they helped him stand and climb the ladder. He squinted in the daylight he hadn't seen in months, and the only flicker of recognition in his eyes came when they emerged from the sugarcane and he saw Proctor Hall just across the yard.

He broke away from the others and ran to the porch of the place that he called home. They were right behind him as he entered the hallway and sat on the fourth riser of the staircase, the spot where he'd sat on the night his family died. And when Marguey Slattery came. He'd sat here on that day too, because this was his spot.

The police wouldn't find Agnes Trimble and her son, Julien, that day. Those two watched everything from the old supervisor's house. They saw the state police car arrive, followed by Landry and Phil. They entered the house and found the girl too. Everything was unraveling at once, it seemed to Agnes.

"You idiot!" Agnes hissed. "You didn't secure the trapdoor. They've escaped and so has she. It isn't safe for us here anymore." She watched Phil and the cops walk into the cane field. They were going to set Noah free.

They could stay no longer. She ordered Julien to go kill April. Now that things were collapsing around them, it was too risky to let her live. He promised to do it and they split up.

THE PROCTOR HALL HORROR

Agnes fled into the swamp. It was a place she knew well, where she had the means to survive and no one would find her. Julien went to his hidden Vespa and drove away. Mother was right about April, but with Landry free, she was all he had left. He decided he'd kill her just as soon as he finished telling her the things he was dying to reveal.

On the way back to New Orleans, Landry told Cate what had happened to him and Phil. When he talked about Agnes instructing her son to kill April, she cried, "Oh God, how can we help her? What can we do?"

There was nothing except to pray for her escape. Julien might already be on the way to where she was being held. With every cop in the state on the lookout, perhaps they'd find him before he could get to her.

"But then what? If he's caught but refuses to tell where she is, she'll die!"

"Maybe not. We have to hope she'll be okay. We don't know where she is or what he's planning. We can only hope and pray."

"What will happen to Noah?" she asked, and Landry pulled to the shoulder.

"With everything else, I never thought about him. There's no way Harry Kanter will leave him in the house alone. They'll put him in a state facility. We can't let that happen. We have to go back."

He called Phil to be sure they were still at Proctor Hall, and twenty minutes later they put Noah in the back seat and once again headed home. They avoided mentioning things about the house or his family, knowing he understood everything.

BILL THOMPSON

They put Noah in the apartment's second bedroom. Landry helped him into the shower and gave him a set of his sweats. Once they were alone, he asked Cate what to do.

She had an idea, and it was a good one. By the time the pizza deliveryman came, she had talked to her father and started planning Noah's future.

CHAPTER FORTY-TWO

Why are these policemen helping me? Always before, policemen hated me. They called me a liar and locked me up. Because I didn't tell them what I had seen, they believed I did terrible things.

When they let me come back home, it was different with my family gone. The man tried to be nice to me, but he couldn't stop the woman from doing bad things. When she killed him, I wondered if she would do it to me next. But instead, she locked me in a box down in that hole. How long has it been? A year? Maybe even longer.

Then those two men were in the hole with me. They talked to me. No one has talked to me in a long, long time. Then the bad one came too, the one they call Julien. He mocked me. He said I was crazy and how did I feel when my family died. No one should ever have that much pain. I lost everything that night.

Who were the men who set me free from that hole today? And the woman. She cares about me.

BILL THOMPSON

The policemen have brought me back to Proctor Hall. Why? What do they want from me? Is it going to start all over again? Are more people dead? Do they blame me for their deaths too?

I will sit in my place on the step and wait. I haven't been in this house in a very long time. I wonder if she's still here. If she has left, then perhaps my family and I can be together again.

CHAPTER FORTY-THREE

As she sat alone for hours with her hands and feet bound, April had cried all the tears she had. Now fear had morphed into resolve. She never considered herself a strong-willed person, but she held the future in her hands. She'd die unless she escaped, so using every ounce of resolve, she tried to create a plan. If he returned — which was becoming less certain as the hours passed — he would kill her, but by God, she wouldn't go without a fight.

By removing her gag last night, he'd proved there was no use screaming because no one was nearby. Now she took in her surroundings. She sat on the floor in a small room with a window and a door. It had rough board walls and floors, and above her were rafters and the roof. The only furnishings were an old chair and a wooden bed frame.

She worked her legs around until she was on her knees, and she stood unsteadily. As she struggled against the ties around her ankles, she shuffled to the window. It was so high on the wall she could barely see out. It was for airflow, not viewing, and when she stood on tiptoe and looked, she saw only green. Tall stalks of sugarcane that surrounded the shack swayed in the breeze. The windowpanes had fallen out ages ago, and she tried shouting, but the cane muffled the sound.

At last April heard a door open and shut, and in a moment the door to her room opened too.

"You're up! I'm glad you're feeling better," Julien said. "I brought you some food." He placed a sack and a plastic drink cup on the floor and snipped off her wrist ties. Despite a sick feeling in her gut, she ate. Escape was her only chance for survival, and to escape she had to maintain her strength.

She held up the wrapper. "So there's a Burger King close by."

"Not close enough for you. We're far from civilization. No one will find you here."

"I have to use the bathroom."

"It's no dormitory restroom, I'm afraid. This place doesn't have running water or indoor plumbing, but there's an outhouse. I'll take you."

When he picked her up and carried her through an adjoining room to the outside, his strength surprised her. It was a warm afternoon, and insects buzzed everywhere in the sea of green stalks. He stood her outside the wooden structure and opened the door. The stench was overpowering, but she had no choice.

"Untie my feet."

"And let you try to escape? Don't be silly. You can do it. Get on with your business."

"At least have the decency to turn around."

THE PROCTOR HALL HORROR

When he did, escape crossed her mind, but it was impossible. What would she do — hop through the cane fields?

She tugged down her pants, held her nose, and squatted over the hole. She thanked God for a roll of paper tied to a nail. She emerged into the sunlight, pulled up her sweats, and said, "Where are we?"

"A long, long way from anywhere. You could scream to high heaven and nobody's around to hear you. It's just acres and acres of sugarcane."

He left more slack in her wrist ties this time, saying, "I don't want to hurt you. I brought you here for your own good."

April held her cuffed hands in the air. "Are these for my own good? Tell me how that works."

"She wants to kill you. If she knew you were here, she'd come to the cabin and do it."

"Who are you talking about? Do you mean the spirit we were talking to through the Ouija board?"

He laughed. "She's no spirit. I'm talking about a living person who'd as soon kill you as not."

She shuddered. "Who is it?"

Julien paused a moment. "You're not going anywhere, so I might as well tell you. I'm talking about Mother."

His mother? *Oh God. Not only is he a raving lunatic, he claims his own mother is a killer.*

"You're lying. How can she hurt me? She's old."

"Perhaps so, but don't underestimate her. I saved your life. Let's leave it at that."

"So you saved my life. Why was that, so you can kill me yourself?"

"I'm not what she is," Julien snapped. "I want someone to talk to — to tell secrets to. You've hardly scratched the surface of Proctor Hall. You may have the psychic power, but ghosts aren't the only things to be afraid of."

"I'm not afraid of ghosts. I'm afraid of *you*."

He shook his head. "I'm on your side. Don't you understand?"

"Didn't you say this has something to do with Landry? Or did I dream it after you slipped me the date-rape drug?"

An idea came to Julien — a way to deal with April instead of killing her. Why hadn't he considered this before? It was perfect!

"It does in fact have something to do with him. Landry will learn firsthand about the Proctor Hall horror. I'll explain everything — I'll walk through the house and show him every detail."

"How? Are you just going to call him up and invite him over? You're a damned kidnapper."

He smiled, creating his plan as they talked. "There's going to be a trade at some point. You for him. Then I'll have him where I want him."

"And if he won't trade?"

"For your sake, you'd better pray he will."

THE PROCTOR HALL HORROR

She stared at him. There was no reason to continue this dialogue when his answers made no sense. She knew one thing only — leaving her fate in this man's hands was tantamount to giving up. She had to survive, and somehow she would.

"I need to sleep," she said, and he walked out. She waited until the outside door closed and she heard a low hum like a small engine. It faded and there was stillness.

She stood, hobbled to the door, and opened it. She went through the only other room, past a rough-hewn table and two chairs standing next to a crude stone fireplace. When she found the front door unlocked, she knew he didn't expect her to escape. Maybe he would be right, but she had to try.

How to get off the low porch was a problem with her feet tethered. If she jumped, she could break a leg or an arm. She sat, slid on her bottom to the edge and swung her feet around. She stood and looked until she saw a break in the cane through which Julien had left.

Without considering what she'd do if he returned, she shuffled off through the tall stalks. They were a foot taller than she, and within seconds she was trapped in a maze that enclosed her on all sides. The barely visible path she'd followed became harder to discern, and soon she realized she had made a serious error. She was lost in a field that might go on for miles. She couldn't even get back to the cabin.

April fell to the ground and wept.

CHAPTER FORTY-FOUR

There was a sound — the same engine noise she'd heard at the cabin — getting closer and closer. She realized she had dozed, sat up, and wondered what to do. Should she cry out for help? What if it was Julien? Should she stay put, safe from him but without water, shelter or protection from predators of the nonhuman kind?

April chose silence, believing he would kill her without hesitation if it suited his purposes. If a coyote dragged her into the woods, it would be no worse than the fate that awaited her.

But it wasn't to be. The sound of the motor grew louder and louder. Then it stopped, and she sat motionless as someone thrashed about.

"April, where are you? You might as well speak up; you can't escape me."

She sat motionless on the ground. As he moved about, she glimpsed him once, but he didn't notice her. A moment later he pulled back the stalks, clicked off a black instrument he held, and put it in his pocket.

BILL THOMPSON

GPS. He put a tracker on me somehow. That's how he found me.

He helped her up, untied her feet, and led her to the little Vespa scooter. He ordered her to walk ahead of him as he pushed it through the field. Back at the cabin, she took another bathroom trip, and then he secured her feet.

"Did you enjoy your adventure?" he asked. She said nothing.

"Escape isn't an option. I'm not an idiot, April. It's a waste of energy to try. Besides, I have stories for you. I want to tell you things about Proctor Hall no one else knows, things I've always had to keep a secret. I can't tell you how much I'm looking forward to it. You enjoyed my course on Louisiana culture, right? This time I'll tell you stories that no college class will ever hear."

He's not worried, she thought. *Once he confides in me, I'll never live to tell his secrets.*

"I have to confess something," he began. "You were destined to choose Proctor Hall for your class project."

"How could that be?" she asked, playing along. If she learned the secrets and then escaped, she could nail this bastard.

"Each year I assign projects, and I ensure one team picks Proctor Hall. It works out well — I lecture about the old house and its mysteries immediately prior to choosing teams. It's fresh on everyone's minds, someone always picks it, and I achieve what I'm after.

"I handpicked your team — you and Andy, Michael and Marisol. I wanted to observe how you and Michael would interact with the two extroverts, and how they would deal

THE PROCTOR HALL HORROR

with each other's egos. Unfortunately, two of them are dead."

She looked up in surprise. "Andy's dead? How do you know that?"

He smiled. "That was hasty of me. I should say he *will* be dead."

Andy will *be dead?* She shuddered as she wondered what he meant.

"At any rate, the four of you trespassed at Proctor Hall, as every team does. You also got into the house, thanks to Cate Adams showing up. That I did not expect, but it was fortuitous and helped propel things forward. Then we learn you're clairvoyant — a truly unexpected pleasure — and you sensed the house's secrets from the first time you entered. That attracted the attention of Henri Duchamp and Landry Drake, both noted ghost hunters. By this time, things were going in an extraordinarily positive direction, far better than in any previous year."

"What secrets are in the old house, and how do you know about them?"

He chuckled. "All in good time. I'm as keen to reveal things as you are to learn about them. That's why every year I've let teams go to Proctor Hall. It was deliciously scary to wonder if they might learn things. What if they discovered the truth about me, for instance — their old college professor who isn't what he seems? It was exhilarating but disappointing too, because none of them thought outside the box. Until you. A clairvoyant in the house at last. I was eager to see what would happen when you put your hands on that Ouija board!"

"So if someone discovered the secrets, would you be in trouble?"

"Trouble doesn't begin to describe what would happen to me. That's why it's so exciting. It's like seeing how close to the precipice one can stand without falling."

"Sounds like you could lose everything. Doesn't that worry you?"

"Ah, you women. You sound just like Mother. Worry, worry, worry."

He mentioned his mother again. This time something clicked — an idea about how he fit into this puzzle.

"You know Proctor Hall so well because you're a Proctor. You're Noah Proctor's brother."

This set him off. "I most certainly am *not* a Proctor. How dare you say that, you impertinent shrew. Enough talk for now." He checked the ties on her hands and feet and stormed out of the room. In a moment she heard the Vespa's engine, loud at first, then faint. He was gone.

With difficulty, April succeeded in getting outside again. Her intention was to look around — to see if there was anything that might help her get free. With a tracker somewhere on her person, it was fruitless to leave. He might get an alert if she left the cabin. No matter what, he'd find her when he returned. She had to think of something else.

She hobbled around the old shack, falling now and then as she shuffled too fast, but managing at last to get around it. As she turned the last corner, she found something useful — a two-inch piece of the cabin's tin roof that had blown off and lay in the dirt.

She had to act fast because he could return at any time. She sat, took the piece of metal in her cuffed hands and began

THE PROCTOR HALL HORROR

to cut through the plastic ties on her ankles. In moments her legs were free, and she maneuvered the piece of tin around and around in her shackled hands, but she couldn't get it positioned.

She tried wedging the metal between two porch floorboards. Now it stuck up like a blade, and she started slicing. Soon she was free of the tethers.

The GPS tracker had to be in her clothing somewhere, but there wasn't time to look for it. She disrobed, taking off everything — outerwear, bra, panties, socks and shoes — and piled them on the porch, hoping the tracker would show she was still at the cabin. Stark naked, she started walking. Which direction didn't matter, because she had no idea where she was. The goal was to get as far from here as possible, find a phone, and call for help.

She walked for a long time and her feet bled from stepping on broken cane stalks. She looked back every so often, glad that the tall stalks closed behind her when she went through. If the tracking device really was in her clothes, Julien wouldn't find her this time.

Her feet were swollen and painful by the time she popped out onto a dirt road. Conscious of her nakedness, she stayed close to the cane, ready to dart back in if she heard the Vespa. She wondered what to do if a car came along. Would they stop for a naked girl? What if she was raped and murdered? Forcing negative thoughts out, she walked down the road until she saw a house. And, thank you God, a line filled with clothes drying in the afternoon breeze.

April crossed the road, ran to the clothesline, and picked off the first thing she found — a sack dress that was too large but served the purpose. She had just pulled it over her head when someone yelled, "Put your hands up, girl."

BILL THOMPSON

A middle-aged woman stood on the porch, aiming a double-barreled shotgun at April. She had seconds to come up with a story, one that didn't involve Julien Girard, because there was no telling who the woman was.

She raised her hands and said, "I'm in trouble. I need help."

"That's a fact, 'cause you stole my dress. I saw you run across the road. What the hell you doing out here bare-ass nekkid?"

April said she'd escaped a kidnapper who took her clothes and would kill her if he found her.

"You came out of the cane field over yonder. That there's the old Girard place."

Yes! Yes, Julien Girard's place! Still afraid, she didn't say his name. She begged to use the woman's phone.

She lowered the shotgun and said, "We ain't got a phone."

"Where's the nearest town?"

"Lockport's five miles away."

"Can you take me there? I need to call someone to come get me."

"Ain't got a car. My husband's in town. He'll be back soon, and if he decides to, he'll take you there. Meanwhile, you come up here and sit on the porch. Don't run off with my dress, you hear? I'd hate to put a hole in it."

The woman's words were mostly bluster, and by the time an ancient pickup pulled into the yard, April had finished a glass of sweet tea. A man wearing dirty overalls got out and came to the porch.

THE PROCTOR HALL HORROR

These were people who lived off the soil — cane farmers, most likely — good people, but wary of strangers. He listened to her story and agreed to take her to Lockport, but only to the police station. And only if she agreed to return the dress once she got her own clothes back.

He let April out in front of the police station and drove away. When he was out of sight, she walked to a 7-Eleven next door. She cajoled the counter man into allowing her to use his phone, and she caught Landry just as he was leaving Channel Nine for the evening. She told him her predicament, said it terrified her that Julien might come around, and asked for help. She said the police station was next door, but what if they knew Julien and someone called him?

It surprised Landry that he'd taken her somewhere near Lockport, his boyhood hometown. He agreed she shouldn't trust anyone, and she had to stay out of sight. Since she had no phone or money, they couldn't communicate further. He told her to find a good hiding place nearby. He would come as quickly as possible and meet her in front of the police station.

Still barefoot and bleeding, April walked across the street into a small park that ran alongside Bayou Lafourche. On a playground she found a plastic treehouse, climbed the small ladder, and crawled inside to wait. She heard a scooter approaching and ducked down, praying it wasn't him. It passed her by, and she looked to see a teenager without a helmet, not her abductor.

Landry called Detective Young, told him where his kidnap victim was, and asked for help. Twenty-five minutes later the whomp-whomp of rotor blades resounded over Main Street in Lockport, and an NOPD helicopter set down in a vacant lot near the police station.

BILL THOMPSON

Landry and Cate stood outside as Young told the local cops he was picking up a lost girl. They came out to watch as the girl emerged from the park, ran to Cate, hugged her and cried, "Thank God. Thank God you're both here."

Half a mile down the highway, a man on a Vespa scooter watched April, Landry, Cate and Detective Young get into the police chopper, rise into the sky and fly away. He might have lost his prey, but she knew nothing that would hurt him. Her escape only made things more interesting, Julien decided as he started the scooter and drove away.

CHAPTER FORTY-FIVE

The chopper flew them to state police headquarters in Baton Rouge, where a medic treated April's swollen feet and a female officer took Cate to Walmart to buy sweats and house slippers for the girl.

They told April what had happened since her abduction. Landry described his, Phil's and Cate's kidnappings and escapes, about finding Noah, and that Julien's mother, Agnes Trimble, murdered Michael. "Julien's a killer too," Landry said, "and I think they're behind a lot of what has happened at Proctor Hall."

April said, "Some of it, but not all. The supernatural entities are everywhere, as you know. Friendly ones and evil ones — you both saw them just like I did. Julien and his mother are a big part of things, but a lot of what happens there is not their doing. There are spirits in that house who want to kill Julien and Agnes."

Lieutenant Kanter ushered them into a conference room. Because the kidnapping happened in Orleans Parish, Shane Young was present too. Cate sat next to April and held her hand. The interview began.

She told them how to find the house where she stole the dress, and how she'd walked naked through a field to get there. She talked about Agnes, who Julien said would kill without compunction. At first she thought Julien might be Noah's brother. But when she asked, he responded as if the Proctors were scum.

Landry said, "He's Ben and Agnes Trimble's son. I don't have to tell you how demented he is. He even killed his stepmother, Mary Girard."

"You're really the one Julien's after," April said to Landry, telling him about the plan to swap her for him. "He says he wants to show you everything about Proctor Hall."

"I hope we can make that happen sometime soon," he replied.

April said Julien intended all along for them to get the Proctor Hall assignment for the class project. It was a total setup, a clever game to find out how close they could come to learning the secrets without uncovering them. He claimed it was a great day when Landry, Cate and Henri got involved.

When she revealed Julien's comment about Andy being dead soon, Landry asked if anyone had heard anything. With so much happening, he hadn't checked on the missing boy.

After the interview, Kanter called Baton Rouge police. He learned the parents had posted a twenty-five-thousand-dollar reward for information, but as of yet they had no word about their son.

The police helicopter took them back to New Orleans. On the way, Cate asked April if she was going back to her parents in Natchez.

THE PROCTOR HALL HORROR

"They want me to, but I have to stay here one more week until the semester is over. I can get an extension on exams, but I can't afford to lose this entire term. School's hard enough for me as it is."

Then came the question of where she'd go tonight. April couldn't return to her dorm room. If Julien was still after her, campus would be the first place he'd look. Instead, Landry and Cate took her to their apartment. The extra bedroom had harbored a person in trouble once before, and they were happy to do it again.

April asked a friend at the dorm to pack some of her things for Cate to pick up later. When the friend asked where April was, she refused to answer because he was still on the loose. Meanwhile, Cate called campus police and arranged for an officer to accompany April when she was at school.

Landry was angry at himself for missing something so basic in his investigation. He had found Joseph and Mary Girard's house in Lockport by searching parish land records. If he'd spent the extra five minutes to search for other records in their names, he'd have found another property — a hundred acres a few miles west of town where the cabin sat.

Lafourche Parish deputies located the cabin by helicopter and tore it apart looking for evidence. Everything was just as April had described it, even the pile of her discarded clothes she'd left on the porch. The cops also found tire tracks from a scooter and pieces of the plastic ties Julien had used to bind her wrists and ankles.

They located the house where April stole the dress. The people said years ago the Girards and many others in the area leased their land to the Lafourche Sugar Cooperative. It wasn't profitable to farm a hundred acres, but when the co-op put thousands of acres together, it worked for everybody.

A block away from April's Tulane dormitory, Julien sat on a motorcycle as Cate emerged with a suitcase. He'd been there most of the day, waiting for one of them to fetch her things, and at last it paid off. The tinted glass on his helmet hid his face as Cate got into the Jeep. He eased the old cycle into traffic behind her and followed at a safe distance.

Campus was the last place anyone would expect to find Julien. Every cop in south Louisiana was looking for him and his Vespa scooter, which sat at the bottom of the bayou like the Corolla.

Some guy in Terrebonne Parish had had the cycle in his yard with a for sale sign on it. He promised it ran great, and Julien paid cash, providing a fake name and address to transfer the title. Proof of ownership was the least of his concerns; getting a new ride would keep the cops off his trail.

He followed Cate downtown and into the French Quarter, pulling to the curb as she went into a parking garage. She carried the suitcase to a building on St. Philip, unlocked the door and went inside. He waited on the street, and a few minutes later Cate and April, each with a longneck beer, stepped out onto a third-floor balcony. He ducked into a shadow as Landry joined them. As he pointed out something on the Mississippi River two blocks away, he looked down St. Philip right past where Julien stood, but he didn't notice a man lurking in a doorway.

Oh, this is excellent! I have all of them in one place.

Julien maintained his post until the apartment went dark around ten. Now he knew where they were, but that could change at any moment. He left to get some much-needed rest, hoping they would be there when he returned.

CHAPTER FORTY-SIX

Before dawn the next morning, Julien was back in a doorway down the block.

The tall doors were open onto the balcony, but the room was dark. As the sun rose, he got curious stares from people who wondered why a man with no ride was wearing a helmet.

"I' a little hot in there?" a teenager smirked, and Julien gave it no thought until a cop walking across the street slowed to look him over. He realized the helmet had the opposite effect from what he intended. While hiding his face, it was also drawing too much attention to him.

He chose an inopportune moment to remove it. Before he could step into a dark recess, Landry appeared in the upstairs window. For a long moment they stared at each other until Landry darted back inside.

Julien sprinted to the corner and made the turn just as Landry hit the sidewalk. Cate was upstairs calling 911, and when Landry didn't see Julien, he incorrectly assumed he'd headed to Bourbon Street to get lost in the crowd. The police were at the apartment when Landry returned, but Julien was already on the interstate and far from the French Quarter.

After they dropped April on campus, Landry and Cate met Henri on the patio outside his office. It was a beautiful morning, less muggy than usual and in the mid-eighties, and were it not for the knowledge that things were far from over, it would have been a perfect day.

Landry said, "Somehow Julien has learned where April is. I saw him across the street this morning, looking up at my apartment. She can't hide forever, but to capture Julien and Agnes, we have to lure them out of hiding. There's only one place to make that happen. I want to conduct another seance at Proctor Hall, and I'll be the bait. Julien said he didn't need April if he had me. Let's give him what he wants."

Henri smiled and said, "Did you intend to ask my opinion about something? So far, all I heard is a statement about what you intend to do."

"He does that a lot," Cate quipped. "Sometimes you just want affirmation, right, darling?" She patted him on the arm as he pulled away in mock anger.

"Okay, if you guys are so smart, come up with something better to flush them out."

"It's a brilliant idea, but risky," Henri began. "I agree with you that's the best place to capture both, but I'm concerned about your safety. If policemen surround the house, your prey won't come out. If you have no protection, they have the element of surprise, and therefore the upper hand."

Cate said, "If the house has hidden places where they can observe what's happening, then you can't involve either of your cop friends. Julien knows both Harry Kanter and

THE PROCTOR HALL HORROR

Shane Young. If he spotted them, he would stay out of sight, and your plan wouldn't work."

"How about we don't involve the authorities? We can all carry weapons — Phil and the camera crew, me, you and Henri…"

Henri threw up his hands. "Don't be silly. I'm no gunslinger. I've never held a weapon, I don't know how to use one, nor do I intend to learn."

Cate said, "You're asking me to use a gun? If Agnes and Julien sneak up on us, what do I do — say 'hands up'? Your idea about a seance may work, but you need to figure out the security aspect, because what you're suggesting is crazy. You're expecting a bunch of amateurs to do the job of the police."

Everyone tossed out ideas and suggestions, and soon Landry left to go to Channel Nine. There was a lot of work to do. Now that they'd accepted his plan, he had little time to execute it. Julien wasn't going away, and Landry had to stop him before he got to April.

Proctor Hall was unoccupied, at least by the living. Noah hadn't been there since the day Cate and Landry took him to New Orleans. She'd called her father with a plan. As a psychiatrist, he agreed that Noah needed a good life instead of a lockup, and he was glad to help.

Doc hired a pilot friend with a Cessna four-seater to fly them to Galveston, and he took over from there. He'd administer psychiatrist evaluations, find a comfortable place for short-term care, and develop a plan for Noah's future.

Back at Proctor Hall once more, the group assembled in the living room for a final seance. Phil had four cameramen, although he didn't expect great footage from two who had no training in photojournalism.

It had been Phil's idea to use cops posing as camera guys. Landry wanted to use state policemen, which meant notifying the sheriff, who wanted his own men. Landry argued that Lafourche was a small parish where everyone knew each other, and Julien might recognize the officers. That made sense to the sheriff, and tonight the state cops with cameras looked like bodybuilders with their Kevlar and guns under street clothes.

A psychic and medium named Madame Blue sat at a table in the center of the room. Henri had hired her, assuring Landry she was a clairvoyant with a good reputation in the paranormal community.

Henri and Landry would sit in chairs and run the planchette on the Ouija board. Against Landry's better judgment, Cate, Doc and Jack watched from the back. The more who were there, the more safety concerns he had, but they insisted.

April, Marisol and a security guard sat with Landry's director and station manager, Ted Carpenter, in a dark room at Channel Nine's French Quarter studio. They would watch a real-time camera feed from Proctor Hall on a giant wall-mounted screen.

Madame Blue had a few instructions. She asked the group to remain quiet and said only she would communicate with the spirits. Landry was curious about her style, as compared to April's quiet and subdued manner. Soon he'd find out just how different tonight would be.

At eight o'clock the medium lit three candles on the table and asked Landry and Henri to put their fingers on the pointer. She started to speak, paused and exclaimed, "The

THE PROCTOR HALL HORROR

spiritual energy in this room is overpowering! Do you feel it?"

Landry did. A tingling sensation ran from his fingers up his arms, but before he could respond, she screamed, "Justice! Peace at last! That's what you want, isn't it? We can help you. Please let us in." Her eyes closed, her head dropped to her chest, and she mumbled in whispers.

In seconds the planchette raced around the board. Henri couldn't keep his fingers on the pointer and concentrate on the letters at the same time. He asked Cate to call out the letters, which were coming at an astounding rate. The pointer zipped around as if it had a mind of its own.

D-I-E-H-E-R-E-E-V-E-R-Y-O-N-E

DIE HERE EVERYONE

As Cate said the words, the psychic's eyes flew open. She raised her hands over the Ouija board and said, "Spirit, reveal thyself. Show us who you are!"

"Holy crap," one of the real cameramen said as a shape appeared beside the mantel — a phantom that appeared as a wispy film of blackness. "See its head?" Landry whispered. "That shows us it's not one of the Proctors."

"We see you," the medium said. "Who are you, spirit?"

A word emanated from every part of the room. It was an uncanny, long and drawn-out moan that was also a name.

Maaaaarrrrrrrryyyyy

Landry said, "Ask if she's Mary Girard."

The wraith nodded and raised its arm toward the door. The planchette jumped to life again, spelling the same words.

BILL THOMPSON

DIE HERE EVERYONE

"Take your fingers off the pointer," the medium said. When Landry and Henri did that, the malevolent ghost in the corner vanished.

Madame Blue closed her eyes again. "Who are you, spirit?"

A new voice answered in a light, tinkling sound. *ME.*

"May Ellen Proctor," Landry whispered.

The medium asked, "May Ellen, do you have something to tell us?"

GO UPSTAIRS AND SEE

A light, airy thing coalesced next to Madame Blue. White gauze covered its torso and arms, and it had no head. May Ellen raised her arm and beckoned, and the group followed, leaving one of the pseudo-cameramen downstairs, pretending to shoot video as he watched for intruders.

The wispy figure floated up the stairs and into a bedroom. The moment they were all inside, the room was plunged into darkness. At first Landry thought the power was off, but lights in the hall behind them shone brightly. In the blackness of the room, a surreal scene unfolded. They were guests at a movie presented by the ghosts of Proctor Hall.

CHAPTER FORTY-SEVEN

The spirit of May Ellen Proctor pointed to the bed, where a person lay sleeping. Loud, eerie snores echoed throughout the room as the wraith turned and pointed to the door behind them.

A dark figure entered the room and crept across the floor to the bed. From under its black robe it drew out a hatchet and decapitated the sleeping person. Blood poured onto the white sheets as the figure in black turned and floated past Landry and the others. It disappeared into the hall.

A surprised cameraman shouted, but Landry shushed him. Now May Ellen moved too, beckoning them to follow her into the hall. When the last person left the bedroom, the lights came back on.

May Ellen took them to the bedroom just across the hall, where the same scene played out before the stunned guests. The lights went out; the black figure entered and decapitated the person sleeping in the bed.

"We are witnesses at the Proctor Hall Massacre," Landry said for the camera. "Julien Girard told me the killer wasn't

BILL THOMPSON

Noah Proctor, so who is the murderer we're seeing at work?" His rhetorical question went unanswered for the moment.

They realized the two already dead were Hiram and Susan Proctor, the parents of May Ellen and Noah. And that meant only one remained — the child whose ghost was taking them from room to room.

The spirit skipped the third bedroom, moving instead to the haunted one across the hall. "That one's Noah's room. There's no one to kill there," Henri whispered.

So many awful things happened in the last bedroom — May Ellen's room. Michael died and Andy went insane there. April called it the most haunted of all.

As the white spirit led them into her own bedroom, Landry spotted another figure he'd missed earlier. Perhaps it wasn't there before. This one hung back from the executioner. This person watched the murderer at work.

Noah, Landry thought. Noah, whose mind was forever warped and twisted by what he saw — and what everyone blamed him for. A wraith went room to room murdering his family, and perhaps he had witnessed every brutal detail.

"Put a camera on that one," Landry whispered to Phil as he pointed.

The black thing entered the room and crept to the bed, but this time things went awry. The child awoke and sat up, screaming in horror as the person raised the hatchet.

"Mommy! Daddy! Noah, help me! Anyone!" Landry looked around and saw the observer standing motionless in the doorway. Could Noah have watched the slaying without rushing to aid his sister? Sadly, that appeared to be what

THE PROCTOR HALL HORROR

had happened. The unfortunate child was doomed. Even her parents couldn't help because they were already dead.

The killer planned it perfectly. Eliminate the adults and save the easiest for last. Did the perpetrator plan to murder Noah next? He had survived, but Landry wondered if they'd find out why.

Just as the black wraith raised its hatchet in the air, May Ellen uttered three words that roared through the room and the house. It was the last frantic plea from a doomed twelve-year-old.

"Agnes! Please don't!"

Landry learned the identity of the killer from the lips of a ghost.

CHAPTER FORTY-EIGHT

Everyone was moved by the tragic scene, but the movie wasn't over yet. Two other figures entered May Ellen's bedroom and joined the killer. They seemed unsure what to do at first, but then they went to work, moving from room to room as a team. Bodies were wrapped in bedclothes, sheets and covers were replaced, and floors scrubbed down. The three worked as one while Noah watched.

BLAME HIM. BLAME HIM.

Those words echoed in the hallway, a succinct explanation as to how a boy who couldn't use words would become the scapegoat. When the trio finished their evil work, Noah walked down the stairs, surveyed the sitting room, and walked to the staircase. He sat on the fourth riser — *his* place — and Landry knew that was where he would stay until the police arrived and blamed him for the bloody massacre.

For a moment after the awful movie ended, no one spoke. They had witnessed a movie that was beyond belief. Even Henri, who had spent decades investigating the paranormal, had experienced nothing like this.

The medium asked them to return to the sitting room, adding, "The dead require our respect. That room symbolizes their sacrifices."

She was right. That room was where Agnes Girard and two others positioned the headless bodies on the couch, placing their heads on the mantel just a few feet away.

They took their places as before, and Madame Blue said, "Thank you, May Ellen. Thank you for showing us what happened. That was a very brave thing you did. Now we will help the police bring the killer to justice."

Landry said, "May I ask her something?"

The medium nodded.

"May Ellen, two others helped Agnes after you were dead. Who were those people?"

B-E-N

"Ben Trimble?"

B-E-N-A-N-D

The pointer stopped. Madame Blue looked up, saw something across the room, and screamed, "Leave us now, evil spirit!"

A dark phantom hovered in a far corner. Had this spirit come to stop the child from uttering its name?

"Mary Girard," Madame Blue whispered. "I feel your presence, Mary. You helped your sister and her husband in this awful crime, and it was your idea to blame poor Noah for everything. Reveal yourself! I command you!"

THE PROCTOR HALL HORROR

The ghost moaned and wailed with drawn-out words.

Nnnnnnoooooooooooo

Landry shouted, "Say you helped them! Admit it, Mary. You're as evil as your sister!"

The specter morphed into human form and raised her arm toward Landry.

Weeeeeee wwwwiiilllll kkkiiilllllll yyyyooooouuuuu

WE WILL KILL YOU

Landry said, "Julien told us insanity ran in your family. You're insane, Mary, but you can't hurt us because Julien murdered you. We're the living. No spirit can touch us."

The medium put her hand on his arm. "You must let me communicate with her. You are not safe here. None of us is."

At that moment from somewhere downstairs arose a horrific wail followed by the sound of a scuffle. The fake cameraman dropped his gear, pulled a pistol from his shirt, and flew down the stairs, with the others close behind. He ordered them to stand back and knelt beside a body in the hallway. They learned what had happened when he pulled a two-way radio from his pants pocket and said, "Ten-double-zero! Repeat, ten-double-zero. Officer down at Proctor Hall!"

The old house had claimed its latest victim. The policeman who'd stayed downstairs lay on the floor, with his head missing and his blood splattered everywhere. A trail of droplets ran down the hallway into the sitting room. When Landry saw them, he knew what they'd find there.

BILL THOMPSON

The harried young cop reacted well to a situation he never expected to face. After that horrific scene upstairs, he discovered his partner's decapitated body. He'd received plenty of training at the academy, but nothing prepared him for killers from beyond the grave. He ordered everyone to wait in the music room while he cleared the house.

His shriek from the sitting room brought everyone running. His eyes wide with astonishment and fear, the cop gagged and pointed to the mantel.

His partner's head stared at them through lifeless eyes.

CHAPTER FORTY-NINE

"You angered the spirits!" Madame Blue shouted at Landry. "Look what they did because you made them mad!"

Everyone — even Cate and Henri — was upset and speaking at once. Through the cacophony, Landry screamed, "Silence! Spirits didn't kill this man. Agnes and Julien are alive, and they are in this house. They're the murderers; let's stay calm and find them."

Sheriff's deputies from Thibodaux heard the radio call reporting an officer down. Four cars with sirens screaming descended upon the house a few minutes before a helicopter dropped into the yard. Lieutenant Kanter and three state cops ran from it to join the others.

After Landry's quick briefing, Kanter barked orders to his men and the deputies, who searched inside and out of the house, looking for the presumptive killers.

From the supervisor's house, Agnes could see the intensive search. If they came near, she would run out the back and disappear into the swamp. For a moment she allowed herself to savor the exhilaration of taking another's life. There was no sensation like it. Even miles away by now, she was certain Julien felt it too.

She hadn't wanted him to leave. As usual, he defied her, and when he called her crazy, she spat at him and said, "Takes one to know one." On that note, he tromped off through the field to find his little scooter. Instead of helping, he left her to take care of the people — and the ghosts.

Julien rode toward New Orleans, weaving between trucks that accounted for most of the interstate traffic at night. His goal was to capture Landry Drake, finish the fascinating discussion that his mother interrupted, and tell the ghost hunter everything about the old house. Afterwards, he'd kill him. He had nothing against Landry, and in fact he enjoyed his company, but it wouldn't be prudent to let him live once he had the answers.

He parked on Decatur again and walked to Landry's building. Landry and Cate were still at Proctor Hall, but not April. Was she up there, just a few feet away? What a tantalizing moment lay in store if he captured her again too. No light came through the tall third-floor windows. She could be asleep, but more likely they'd sent her somewhere safe. *From me,* he chuckled.

Julien took a chance. He went to the building's door, examined the lock, and thanked the historical commission for making owners preserve the past. The ancient lock took less than a minute to pick. Landry's apartment had a modern lock, but it too yielded to the instrument Julien used.

Once inside, he searched the rooms. No one was here. He resisted the temptation to go through their personal things and learn more about the things they liked and read and wore. Instead he sat on the living room couch in the dark,

THE PROCTOR HALL HORROR

his .38 pistol in his lap and a switchblade in his pocket. They would return sometime, and when they did, he would be ready.

CHAPTER FIFTY

His head bobbed now and then as he struggled to stay awake. Sitting in the dark with nothing to do but wait wasn't conducive to keeping one's mind on things, but this could be the most important night of Julien's life.

Much time passed before he heard something. He crept to the door, put his ear to it, and heard footsteps. Voices too — Landry and Cate had returned, and at last things could begin! He flipped off the pistol's safety and waited behind the door.

A key went into the lock, the tumbler turned, and the door opened a bit. "I'll be fine from here. Thanks for making sure I got back safely. If Landry and Cate aren't already home, they'll be here soon."

He listened as April said goodbye to whoever walked her home. He smiled. As much as they tried to keep her safe, it hadn't worked.

———

Landry, Cate, Doc and Henri didn't leave Proctor Hall until well after midnight. After Channel Nine's crew left and the cops finished their fruitless search, they stayed another hour with Lieutenant Kanter and the sheriff. The cops had interviewed everyone, but Kanter wanted the opinions of Landry and Henri, the paranormal experts.

The sheriff knew Kanter and Landry had worked together, but the veteran state cop didn't bat an eye when Landry mentioned spirits and Ouija boards, wailing ghosts and headless corpses. The sheriff didn't believe in such things, but watching Kanter listen to the hair-raising tales gave him reason to doubt his beliefs. He was born and raised in this parish and thought he knew every story about Proctor Hall. Today he learned how much he didn't know.

"I've sent men to the sugar mill and the cabin outside Lockport," Kanter said. "Any other ideas where the killers might have gone?"

Henri said, "We shouldn't ignore the possibility they're still here in the house. They moved about undetected, murdered a police officer, and disappeared in seconds. It appears they watched our movements, which means there may be more hidden passages." He showed the cops the ones they'd found earlier, and the sheriff ordered his men to keep looking for hidden rooms. When Landry left, they were knocking and banging on floors, walls and corners.

Kanter told Doc he'd lock up when they left, and Landry and the others headed back to New Orleans. He dropped Doc at his hotel and Henri at his office, parked the car, and they walked home.

When he opened the door to his apartment and flipped on the light, Cate screamed. April sat on the couch across the room. Plastic ties bound her wrists and ankles, and there was duct tape over her mouth. With eyes wide, she glanced hard to the left as they ran to help her.

THE PROCTOR HALL HORROR

"She's trying to tell you someone is hiding behind the door," Julien said, closing it. "We've been waiting for you. I'm so glad you're all here. It's time to tell you everything about Proctor Hall."

CHAPTER FIFTY-ONE

With his weapon pointed at Landry and Cate, Julien told her to remove the duct tape from April's mouth. He ordered them to sit on the couch with April, tossed plastic ties to Cate, and said, "Hook Landry's wrists together. Not too tight, but don't try to fool me. I'll check your work when you're done." Next came his ankles, and then he told Cate to stand facing away from him and put her hands behind her back.

He had to use two hands, and when Landry saw him put the gun on a table, he nodded at Cate. She whirled, caught Julien off guard, and brought her knee up hard between his legs. He cupped his groin and fell to the floor in agony.

She grabbed the pistol, keeping it trained on Julien as she backed to a drawer, took out scissors, and cut the ties from Landry's wrists. He freed his legs and took the gun while Cate released April, who shivered from fright after hours in the dark with him.

"Call Harry," Landry said, and Cate got him on the line. He promised to send NOPD to the apartment and join them as soon as he could get to New Orleans.

Landry tossed the plastic strips to Julien and told him to bind his ankles. Julien took the ties and looked at his feet, but in one swift move he pulled his switchblade from an ankle holster, flipped it open and seized April. He put the knife to her throat and threatened to kill her if Landry didn't drop his weapon.

"You know I have nothing to lose. I'll get the death penalty for what I've done. One more murder won't make my sentence any harsher. Put the gun down now or shoot me. But I'll kill her before I die."

There were sirens and the sound of screeching tires from the street below. "We're out of time," Julien snapped, running the razor-sharp knife over her neck and drawing blood. "Do you want her death on your hands?"

"You won't kill her," Landry said as they heard the cops breach the street door to the building two stories below. "And you don't want to die either. You have a story to tell. Ever the academic, Dr. Julien Girard, professor of history. Put down the knife, take your medicine, and I promise you we'll all go back to Proctor Hall so you can tell us the rest."

Cate held her breath at this dangerous tactic. Julien paused, but as heavy footsteps banged up the stairway and someone yelled, "Police! Open the door!" he dropped the knife on the floor, and Landry scooped it up.

She unlocked the door, and three uniformed officers stormed inside, assessed the situation, and in seconds Julien Girard was in custody at last.

The next morning they met at Henri's office. He was aghast at what had happened after he left them, and he said Landry had no obligation to keep his promise to Julien. It was a desperate move to keep a girl from dying. Julien was safely in jail, and in jail he should stay.

THE PROCTOR HALL HORROR

Cate's father played devil's advocate. "First off, nobody's certain if Landry can make good on his promise. It'll be a miracle if you convince the state police to allow Julien back there. But you've pulled a rabbit or two out of a hat before. So let's say we do go. Let's think about what we still don't know. There's the truth about Noah, Agnes and the rest of them. Where the bodies are buried. How many more secrets there are and what happened to Marguey Slattery. We need answers, and Julien will tell us. I say we should give it a shot. Let's try to get him back to Proctor Hall."

"How about you?" Landry asked Cate.

She smiled. "How long have I known you? Years, right? And how many times have I been right when I warned you about something? Always, right? And how many times have you gone off anyway and done things your way? Always, right? I rest my case."

Everyone chuckled, and Landry agreed there was an element of risk involved, but with Julien shackled and with sufficient firepower, what could go wrong?

Cate shook her head. "See what I mean? Put enough sugar on a turd and it looks like a chocolate eclair. The only thing that could go wrong is that Proctor Hall is a hotbed of supernatural activity. There are ghosts in there — not Casper, but the bad kind. Shackles, cops, guns — those things are useless against the paranormal."

She exhaled a long sigh and said, "So how soon are you thinking we should go?"

CHAPTER FIFTY-TWO

Moving a prisoner charged with multiple capital crimes and held without bail proved to be less difficult than Landry expected. Julien Girard was allowed to leave prison under heavy guard for one reason only — a high-level career officer also wanted him back there — Lieutenant Harry Kanter.

Landry and Harry had opposite motives but similar goals. Both wanted answers. For Landry it would wrap a story that would be his next *Bayou Hauntings* episode. Harry wanted to learn how many more people Julien and his relatives had disposed of. With Julien's information, they might find bodies and solve decades-old cold cases.

The sheriff knew Kanter was no novice about supernatural phenomena. While working with Landry, he'd become a believer in the powerful entities that existed beyond the realm of understanding. He was also a pragmatist — a cop whose stock in trade were pistols and handcuffs and interrogations. He believed with enough officers and firepower, he could take his prisoner to Proctor Hall and bring him back without incident, paranormal activity be damned.

Today they would test that theory. Two marked state police cars traveled from Baton Rouge to Lafourche Parish. Kanter, Julien and two officers rode in one. Four cops rode in the other — in all, six of the finest and best-trained men on the Louisiana State Police force. They carried semiautomatic weapons, stun grenades and tear gas.

From the other direction came the WCCY-TV van with Landry, Cate, Henri, Doc and Landry's crew — Phil Vandegriff and three camera guys. As before, Marisol and April would follow the camera feed from the station. Landry had asked for that — it was the least they could do after the harrowing experiences April had endured.

Rain came down hard as the vehicles turned off Highway 308 down the narrow lane to Proctor Hall. The day held threats of thunderstorms, but Harry's permission to remove prisoner L-308475 was for twelve hours only, and the clock had begun ticking ninety minutes ago when Julien left the state lockup in Baton Rouge.

In less than an hour, the cameras had been placed and things were ready. They planned to shoot four hours of footage or less. Landry had five more hours for contingencies such as unexpected issues or a trip to Lockport.

Julien remained in the police car until it was time. Two cops took him by the arms and helped him shuffle along in the rain to the front porch. He wore bulky leg irons and hands cuffed in front, and the officers helped him maintain his balance.

Landry gave a brief statement for the camera and said, "Julien, are you ready to show us the secrets?"

The former professor nodded and smiled. As it turned out, he had prepared an opening statement of his own.

THE PROCTOR HALL HORROR

"I won't be going back to Baton Rouge today. Landry and Henri, you both know that Proctor Hall is where I belong. These policemen think restraints are a deterrent to the entities who inhabit this house, but you two know what I'm saying."

Lieutenant Kanter said, "Julien, you're full of shit. I promise you you're going back to jail. There's nothing you can do to avoid it."

"Tell him, Landry. Tell him how foolish that thinking is."

"Let's get this started," Kanter muttered. "We're on the clock, and I'm tired of your rhetoric."

Landry had confidence that the officers could handle crises, but Julien's words concerned him. His statement was correct — ordinary boundaries didn't apply to the supernatural. He wondered if he'd made a serious mistake by bringing the man here.

Flanked by officers, Julien led them into the music room. He showed them where to pull back the carpet and see an almost-invisible seam in the flooring that marked the way Agnes had gotten into the house unobserved. "There's a latch on the bottom," he explained. "From outdoors she goes beneath the house, opens the door, and sneaks inside."

Landry had examined that very section of floor himself and had missed the tiny seam. He wondered what else they'd overlooked.

In the hall, Julien opened a door to a broom closet and pointed. "Behind that back panel is an air shaft that runs up into the left bedroom on the bayou side. There's a ladder on the wall."

Landry said, "That's May Ellen Proctor's room, the one where Michael died. Since you mentioned it, I have some questions. Why don't we go to the kitchen and talk?"

An enormous clap of thunder shook the walls of Proctor Hall. The lights flickered as the cops helped Julien into a chair at the kitchen table.

Landry said, "Tell me about Michael. In just minutes, you ended up in the bed with his corpse. I want to know how and why you killed him and where the murder weapon is."

"I regret that incident. It's something for which I am truly sorry. Agnes killed him — she hid in the air shaft, hoping to catch one of us in the bedroom alone. Michael entered, she crept up behind him, sliced off his head, and he fell onto the bed. His head — as Landry's aware — landed on the floor."

He brushed away a tear, leaving Landry to wonder why this one of his atrocities seemed to affect him while others didn't.

Julien continued, "I pulled back the curtain and saw what she had done. She didn't have to kill an innocent boy — my student — but that was why she did it. She was reminding me I wasn't really a professor. Deep inside my psyche lives a demon, just like the one inside hers. I saw poor Michael, lost consciousness, fell on his bloody corpse, and awoke when you called my name. She keeps the hatchet somewhere in the house, close at hand for when she needs it, but I'm not aware where. Someday you may find it."

Although Landry didn't trust him, the answer made sense. Surprised at Julien's willingness to bare his soul, Landry began to think they might get the answers they sought at last.

CHAPTER FIFTY-THREE

Before they left the kitchen, Henri opened the pantry and said, "Were you going to tell us about the hidden stairway in there?"

"Ah, so you already found that one. I don't consider it a secret, and I forgot about it. It was a functional part of the house. The servants could go to the master bedroom without taking the front stairs. You find this often in these old homes."

Landry pressed on. "Where are the members of the Proctor family buried?"

"Here. Here in the house. Agnes said Ben took care of that."

Lieutenant Kanter interjected, "Exactly where in the house?"

"They're entombed in the walls, a constant reminder of what my mother did at Proctor Hall. I don't know exactly where, but Agnes said they were here, and I believe her."

"I don't believe you," Kanter said. "That makes no sense. If you put a body in a wall in this humidity, it won't be long before you have an awful stench."

"My mother said Ben built crude wooden coffins, put them in, and packed them with lime. He had plenty of that; there were bags of it stored at the mill. He nailed the lids on, stood the boxes upright in the walls, and paneled over them. Same thing with Joseph Girard. When he died here at Proctor Hall, Ben took care of him the same way."

Landry said, "Tell me how Ben died."

"Another sad ending," Julien answered, although his face displayed no emotion. "Six years ago, Agnes escaped the cage one last time. She caught Ben by surprise, bludgeoned him to death with a hammer, and dragged his body underneath the house." He looked at Kanter. "I'm expecting your next question, Lieutenant. She didn't use lime or a box. She just left him there. I guess she knew the animals would take care of him before the smell gave away his whereabouts. And not long after that, everyone left Proctor Hall anyway."

The more Julien described the heinous crimes in such casual terms, the more repulsed Cate became. As everyone walked upstairs to the bedrooms, Cate stayed back. She wandered down the hall, trying to distance herself from the insanity. Her eye caught movement as she passed the sitting room, and she took a step back.

In front of the fireplace floated the white, wispy phantasm that was May Ellen Proctor. Cate walked toward her, experiencing warmth and goodness after the awful revelations just in the next room.

"I'm glad to see you," she said, and the figure shifted. There was a sound — just the slightest hint of a melodic tinkle and a drawn-out whisper of a word.

THE PROCTOR HALL HORROR

DANGER.

There came another rumble of thunder as the dim light from a single ceiling fixture cast eerie shadows throughout the room where the bodies once sat.

"Are we in danger, May Ellen?"

COMING FOR YOUUUUUUUU.

At that instant a bolt of lightning struck the top of the house, plunging Proctor Hall into darkness. Suddenly in this room the gloom was palpable. Here was a medley of evil, memories of unspeakable deeds, spirits longing to break free, phantoms seeking revenge, and insane horrors yet to come.

Cate couldn't breathe. As she gasped, her chest constricted and the air wouldn't come. She stumbled into the hall and fell to the floor. She looked up to see a woman standing over her. There was an aura of hatred around her. Cate wondered if it was real or just an illusion. She felt dizzy and fell unconscious to the floor.

"Cate, can you hear me? Cate! Where are you?"

She opened her eyes and took a moment to orient herself. She was lying on a hard floor in the dark.

Proctor Hall. I fainted. Danger. We're in danger.

I hear my name.

"I'm here, downstairs in the hall!"

She heard footsteps on the stairs, and then Landry knelt by her side. "I lost you for a moment," he said, holding her hand. "I thought you were with us. Are you all right?"

She sat up, letting the blood flow to her brain and clear her thoughts. "I saw May Ellen. She told me we're in danger. They're coming for us."

"Who are they?"

"I don't know. Why is it so dark in here?"

"It's the storm. The guys have lights upstairs. Come on, let me help you stand."

Henri shouted for Landry. "Hurry. Things are happening!"

Everyone was in what they called the haunted bedroom, although Landry thought that applied to every room in the house. The camera lights provided narrow beams of illumination; most of the space lay in darkness, punctuated by the occasional jagged streak of lightning through the windows.

Grim specters tore and dove like blackbirds through the air above May Ellen's bed. Groans and sighs filled the room, and it was impossible to miss the overpowering sense of doom. Things were building to a climax. Landry grew anxious but resisted ordering everyone to leave. He wanted a little more footage — a few more shots of supernatural activity.

As Cate watched from the back of the room, the familiar white figure materialized beside her. With every sighting, May Ellen's ghost assumed more form and substance. Now Cate could see details of the lace on her white dress and her bare feet. She avoided looking at the top, where her head should have been.

"Should we use the Ouija board?" Cate whispered to her.

The spirit moved as if wafting in a summer breeze.

THE PROCTOR HALL HORROR

NO, the specter said in its melodious voice. As before, she drew out the word until it became a whisper.

THEY WANT HER.

"Who?"

THE BAD ONES WANT HER.

Julien stood rigidly as the phantoms swirled about him. Lieutenant Kanter held his arm in a viselike grip, determined not to let go no matter what happened. Despite his intention, the wild activity that came at him from everywhere distracted the cop. He swatted as an ominous shadow swept across his face, lost his balance, and crashed to the floor.

"Leave Julien alone!" came a shout from somewhere. Landry recognized the voice.

Obeying the command, the black masses disappeared in seconds. "That's Agnes, Julien's mother!" Landry shouted. "Quick! We have to find her." He, Cate, Henri and Doc ran out into the hall.

Kanter yelled that Julien was missing. The cameramen directed their lights around the room until the lieutenant found his prisoner hiding under May Ellen's bed. The other cops pulled him out and slammed him into a chair.

There was no luck finding Agnes in this house so familiar to her. Landry presumed she used another hidden space Julien had neglected to mention.

"Why did the spirits obey her command?" he asked Julien.

"It's not me they're after. They're using me to get to her. They want her, and they're determined to keep you and the police from getting to her before they do."

"Are you talking about the Proctors?"

"No. Ben Trimble, for one. There's something I haven't told you that will better explain things. Ben and Agnes Trimble were husband and wife, and they are my parents. But they're also first cousins. Agnes's maiden name was Trimble, and so was Mary Girard's. When I say insanity is in my genes, I'm not exaggerating. All three of them were lunatics, and the Trimbles' only child got a double dose.

"The ghosts of Hiram and Sarah Proctor want Agnes to die a horrible death. They're not evil spirits, but they harbor a deadly animosity toward her. She murdered them and blamed everything on their helpless son, Noah."

Landry asked if there were others.

"My stepmother, Mary. She's as evil as Agnes, and she wants me because I murdered her. So far Agnes has kept her in check, but Agnes is getting old, and her power to control the spirits is fading. Given the chance, Mary will kill me."

"Yet you still agreed to come back to Proctor Hall?"

Julien nodded. "I have nothing to lose. All this has to end — for me, my mother, Noah, all of us, living or dead. Proctor Hall had to give up its secrets someday, and if Mary Girard kills Agnes and me, then so be it. Maybe that's how it's meant to turn out. For me, I don't plan to walk out of this house alive."

Kanter said, "You'll be leaving upright if I have anything to do with it."

THE PROCTOR HALL HORROR

"But that's the rub, Lieutenant. You have nothing to do with it. You're powerless against the forces in this house."

CHAPTER FIFTY-FOUR

Just then Doc Adams said, "Landry, do you smell something?"

He took a deep breath. "Smells like rotten eggs."

"I think so too. Everybody stop what you're doing! Don't touch anything. It's a gas leak. Get out of here fast. If the electricity comes back on, it can blow the house up."

From the sitting room, Agnes listened to the shouts as they raced down the stairway and out the front door. They started the car engines; they wouldn't go far, but turning on the kitchen stove burners had bought her a little time. She heard footsteps on the stairway and ran to hide, but stopped at the sound of Julien's voice.

"Mother, they forgot about me! Help me get to the blacksmith shop. I can use the tools to break my chains."

The old shop lay across the front yard alongside Bayou Lafourche. She said, "Everyone is on the other side of the house. I can't risk going with you, but you can make it if you try. I know you can do it, son." She helped him to the porch and returned to the house.

He stumbled down the porch steps, fell into the grass, and did a slow crab-walk across the yard toward the ruined blacksmith shop.

On the back side of Proctor Hall, Phil and the cops moved the vehicles away from the house. When they regrouped, Landry asked who had Julien.

"Shit!" Kanter said. "Shit, I had him, and in the craziness I left him. He's still in the house! I've got to go back."

Landry grabbed his sleeve, but the cop pulled away and started running.

Agnes walked down the hall and into the kitchen to turn off the gas flowing from the open burners. Her eyes stinging from the noxious fumes, she took a deep breath, ran across the room, and turned them off.

At that precise, fateful moment, the lights came on inside Proctor Hall.

The last moment of Agnes Girard's life came when the ceiling light fixture illuminated, followed in milliseconds by a thunderous noise and a brilliant flash of light. The kitchen walls exploded outward, as did May Ellen's haunted bedroom above it.

On the opposite side of the house, Harry Kanter almost made it to the porch. Running full speed, the impact knocked him to the ground. Every window on this side exploded, sending shards of glass flying into the yard, and he drew his weapon as he wondered what happened.

Within minutes the rainstorm had doused the flames, and by the time the Thibodaux Fire Department trucks arrived,

THE PROCTOR HALL HORROR

a thick cloud of black smoke rose into the gray sky. From the back side where Landry and the others had parked, Proctor Hall appeared untouched except for its windows. The building was three-quarters intact. Only a corner of the bayou side had been ripped away; a gaping hole yawned where the kitchen and May Ellen's bedroom once stood.

In an instant Channel Nine's crew was part of a major news event. The van they'd brought was equipped for remote feed, and soon they were broadcasting live footage from Proctor Hall with Landry Drake as the reporter.

When a state arson investigator arrived, Doc told him about smelling natural gas and getting everyone out in the nick of time. But not quite everyone, they learned. A firefighter searching debris in the yard shouted, "There's a body out here!" The corpse of an elderly woman, barefoot and wearing work clothes, lay in the wet grass a hundred feet from the house. She had been ejected so quickly that not even an eyebrow was singed. Landry felt certain this was Agnes Trimble, but until identification could be made, she would be called Jane Doe.

Humidity hung in the air after the drenching rain, and fog shrouded the banks of Bayou Lafourche just a hundred yards away. Landry thought he saw something in the grass near the water — a pile of black rags, or maybe something that had swept up from the bayou in the storm.

He ran across the lawn, stopping short when he saw movement. It looked like a pile of black clothes, but as he moved closer, a head popped up and he realized what he was seeing.

A phantom was crouched on the ground, its black shroud hiding its face until Landry drew close and looked into the eye sockets of the skull that leered at him. There was something else — something on the ground under the specter's shroud. As he moved closer, the phantom flew into the air, soared toward the bayou, and disappeared into the fog.

"I need an EMT over here!" he yelled as he knelt beside the mangled body of Julien Girard.

As the others gathered, the medical team brought their equipment and went to work. "Julien, can you hear me?" Landry said. As despicable as he was, no one deserved this.

"Yesssss," a hoarse growl issued from his bleeding throat. The creature had gouged hunks of flesh from his face. His cheekbones were visible, and just a flap of skin connected his nose to his face.

"His blood pressure's dropping fast," a tech said. "I'll call for a medivac."

"Julien, what happened?" Landry asked, holding his cold, clammy hand.

"Tried to get to…blacksmith shop…remove chains…she crawled up out of the bayou…"

"What was that thing?"

"Mary…thought I killed her…guess she finally got me."

Mary Girard, his insane stepmother.

The medical examiner walked back across the yard and shouted, "Who the hell moved the body?"

Landry could barely see the man through the thick fog. "What are you talking about?"

"The dead woman that was over here. Who moved the body?"

THE PROCTOR HALL HORROR

Landry ran to where he stood. The indentation in the grass was unmistakable. The body had been there, but in the short time they'd tended to Julien, it had disappeared. They questioned everyone and searched the house and grounds, but no one would ever find Agnes Girard's body.

CHAPTER FIFTY-FIVE

Landry visited Julien in the hospital a few brief times. With his face swathed in bandages and under heavy sedation, the man wasn't aware of the visits. Landry understood that; he came out of pity for the tormented man.

Once Julien awoke, Lieutenant Kanter would post an officer outside his door. For now the man didn't pose a flight risk. He started out in ICU, followed by a round of surgeries. A plastic surgeon reconstructed his damaged face and grafted skin where the phantom's fingernails had torn away his flesh. He returned to ICU after that, and later to a regular room. Lengthy rehabilitation lay ahead.

Kanter wanted to interview Julien as soon as possible. At last the doctors slowed down the sedatives and allowed a ten-minute visit twice a day. Kanter drove down from Baton Rouge for the first session and asked Detective Young to conduct the rest. That would save Kanter a lot of driving.

Landry asked to attend the sessions and bring Phil to video them. Kanter had no issue with it, since the recording would act as a permanent record and allow him to watch the sessions he missed.

On the morning of the first session, they waited outside the door while a nurse roused Julien and told him there were visitors. He recognized Landry and Phil, and he nodded when Landry reminded him Harry was a state cop.

Landry asked how he felt, and Julien touched the bandages on his face. "It's painful beyond belief. The doctors had a lot to fix. She ripped my face apart, and she'd have torn my body to shreds if someone hadn't come. Perhaps that would have been best for everyone."

Kanter said with only ten minutes, the small talk must wait. Julien had been Mirandized earlier, but the cop read his rights again for the record.

Kanter pulled a notepad from his pocket. "There are some loose ends about Proctor Hall I'd like to ask you about in what little time we have. I need as much information as you can provide. What happened to Marguey Slattery?"

Julien spoke in a hoarse whisper. "Marguey. A girl in the wrong place at the wrong time. Ben and Agnes and Noah lived at Proctor Hall then. One day I drove over in the rain to see them. Noah sat on the stairs like he always did. My parents and I sat on the porch and talked. She fixed a pitcher of sweet tea. I will never forget my thought that this is how normal families interact. No insanity or killing or mayhem — just three people looking out toward the bayou in the rain.

"Poor Marguey came along in her pirogue and tied up to a tree. Nobody said a word, but we saw the spirit materialize in the yard. That damned May Ellen Proctor waved to her. She floated down toward the bayou, and the girl in the boat screamed when she realized May Ellen was a ghost.

THE PROCTOR HALL HORROR

"We ran down there and everything started happening. Agnes and Ben grabbed Marguey out of the boat and dragged her up to the house. She dropped her hat on the porch — that's how her father realized later she'd been there. They took her inside and let Noah be blamed for her disappearance, just like at the massacre."

Kanter asked, "And you? What did you do while this kidnapping was underway?"

A nurse entered the room. "Time's up, I'm afraid," she said. "Mr. Julien needs his rest now."

"Let him answer," Kanter said, but the nurse wouldn't budge.

"A deal's a deal. The doctor told you ten minutes twice a day. Time's up. Now go."

"I'll see you this afternoon," Landry said as they walked toward the door.

Julien croaked, "Lieutenant, I was as happy as they to have a new victim after all those years. I'm insane. There's no cure for me. All that awaits me is eternity in hell."

"Why do you care about that bastard?" Kanter asked as they walked to the parking garage. "You treat him like he's your friend."

"Even a monster deserves compassion. He's still a human being. Imagine the conflict of living a lie for decades. He's been a typical college professor on the outside and a demented madman within. I think confessing is cathartic for him, like a cleansing ritual. He's not asking for forgiveness or understanding. He wants to tell someone his story before it's too late."

Kanter left his list of questions with Landry, and in the afternoon session, Detective Young confirmed Mary Girard was the specter who attacked Julien at Proctor Hall.

He said, "I told you she wanted to get to me. She wants revenge. When she attacked me, she whispered, 'You threw me in the bayou while I was still alive.' Do you understand what that means? I swear I wouldn't have thrown her in there if I'd known she wasn't dead. I saw the gators thrashing around. They killed Mary, not me."

"Any remorse?" the cop asked, and Julien shook his head.

"I wish I weren't like this. God knows I wanted to be normal. I didn't want the woman who raised me to die like that. But am I sorry for what I did? No. I'll do it again, given the chance. I'm beyond help. I'm beyond everything that's decent."

"Where's Agnes?" Julien asked, and Landry realized he hadn't heard about the explosion. When he said Julien's mother had died, the man muttered, "About time." Landry said her body vanished soon after her death, and Julien suggested perhaps the ghostly Proctor family claimed her body.

They learned that he faked Noah Proctor's death certificate to protect his mother, Agnes. With Noah dead, she didn't have to worry about anybody from social services or the mental health system checking up on him. After she killed Ben in 2014, she began keeping Noah in that upstairs cage that had been hers. Neither that nor anything else bothered Noah, but at last she had to leave.

"Occasionally curious people came to see the haunted mansion. Agnes would hide, but some of them went inside, and luckily none was alone. She'd have killed again, but at her age, she couldn't attack more than one. She created

THE PROCTOR HALL HORROR

spooky sounds to scare off intruders, and fortunately for her, nobody ever went upstairs and found Noah."

Landry said, "But why keep Noah alive at all? It was a burden for her."

"Even in her eighties, she still had an insatiable desire for murder. Noah was her hole card. If the opportunity arose and she caught an unfortunate victim in Proctor Hall, she could bring Noah out, sit him back on the stairway, and let the police find him. Everyone in the parish would have thought Noah did it."

Their time ran out, and Landry offered to buy Shane a beer. Young returned to the precinct station, wrapped up a few things, and met Landry and Cate at Harry's Corner on Dumaine. There are people who've interacted with cops enough to recognize one even in street clothes. When Young walked in, some guys at the bar held up their hands and yelled, "Raid! Down on the floor!" Everyone found that hilarious, including Shane.

Cate listened as they discussed the interview with Julien. In her mind, the man had no conscience. Insanity was a catchall word for many flaws, and poor Julien — who declared himself insane — had inherited more than his share of bizarre amorality. Doomed from birth, it surprised Landry how resigned about his fate he appeared to be.

That evening Landry got a call from the duty nurse, who advised them they couldn't meet with Julien tomorrow. He'd developed a low-grade fever and his heart rate was elevated, and the doctor had put him on antibiotics and a sedative to let him sleep.

After he texted Detective Young to cancel the meeting, Cate reminded him that tomorrow demolition would begin at Proctor Hall. With the house damaged beyond repair, her father had hired a demolition firm. Forensic experts from the state police would work beside the wrecking crew as they removed walls, floors and ceilings.

Since Landry had committed to attending Julien's interviews, he had to miss the demolition. With free time now, he was excited to go along.

"I'll call Phil and have him come record everything," he said. "And Henri. We should ask Henri too."

She smiled. "We already have. You're not the only organized one in this household. Phil and Henri will be there too."

"What would I do without you?" he quipped.

"Lord only knows. I wonder that myself sometimes."

Hours later, Julien called Landry's direct line at WCCY-TV and left a voicemail. In a weak voice, his words came between gasps for air. Julien could have reached Landry on his cell, but as Landry and Cate listened, they realized he wanted to make a statement instead of having a conversation.

"I want to explain about April. It was wrong to abduct her, but I did it for the right reasons. I needed someone to confide in. The things I had done ate me up inside, and with her psychic abilities, I believed we had a connection. Agnes would kill April to keep me from telling her things, so I hid her at the cabin in Lockport. Mother would have found her at Proctor Hall. I hope you can understand that not everything I've done in my miserable life was bad. I wanted to save her life."

In Cate's opinion, the statement was a pathetic attempt to justify a kidnapping. It was the last straw for her. She had no more empathy for this monster.

CHAPTER FIFTY-SIX

The next morning Landry, Cate and Phil drove to Thibodaux. On the way he called the hospital and spoke to a nurse who advised him Julien was now in ICU. When Landry asked what had happened, she said she couldn't release patient information, although Lieutenant Kanter had called earlier. "Since Mr. Girard's a prisoner, I gave him a patient update. You might check with him."

Kanter said Julien's temperature had spiked during the night. He had so much difficulty breathing that he had been put into an induced coma and was on a ventilator. His doctor believed he had sepsis.

"He may have given us all we'll get," Kanter said. Landry said he was going back to the house, and Kanter asked him to check in. His own men would be there, but he wanted Landry's point of view on the situation.

Landry played Julien's voicemail for Phil. He agreed with their conclusion last night. It sounded like a last-ditch attempt by a desperate man to clear his name if not his conscience. Cate wished she could find something decent about the man, but after hearing his confessions, she had no room in her heart for his protestations.

When they arrived at Proctor Hall, they found two state police crime scene vans parked next to a beautifully restored red 1990 Jaguar XJ6. Landry smiled. Henri had brought his baby out for a drive. He couldn't remember the last time that had happened.

Several trucks and machines marked "Christian Brothers Demolition" sat in the yard, and a team of men and women in hard hats waited for instructions. They had examined the structure and determined parts of the second floor were unsafe because of the blast. Starting with the kitchen, they would move through the house, striving to maintain structural integrity until it was time to bring the place down. The medical examiner's people would work alongside the demo team.

A few days earlier, movers had cleaned out the house. They moved all the furniture and personal items to a warehouse Doc owned in Metairie so someone could examine them. The house had plenty of secrets, and Landry hoped perhaps even the furnishings might give up something interesting.

Cate gave the order to begin, and what had been a peaceful scene became a beehive of activity. The medical team and the workers climbed up from the yard into the ruined kitchen. Phil donned a hard hat and joined them while Landry, Cate and Henri watched from the yard a few feet away. The workers tossed lumber into a pile in the grass, where a crane with a huge metal scoop would transfer it to a dump trailer.

They made quick work of the kitchen because it was just a shell. Nothing interesting turned up in what remained of its walls and floors.

THE PROCTOR HALL HORROR

The demolition crew moved to the downstairs hall, signaled that things seemed structurally sound, and the show moved inside. Landry and the others entered the house through the back door and watched from the far end of the hall as the men took crowbars to the wall panels and worked their way down the halls, ripping them off. Nothing lay behind them except the rough-hewn studs and crude insulation used in 1910 when Mason Proctor built the house.

The first discovery came when they removed the walls that covered the underside of the staircase. One of the inlaid panels proved to be a door. Henri moved closer for a look, showing the others how a latch would release when someone pressed a certain place. Boxes containing handwritten ledgers filled the tight space.

Landry hoped they would reveal secrets about the house and its occupants, but they served a more monotonous purpose. As the crew removed dozens of boxes, Landry selected two from the 1920s at random and found meticulous entries that chronicled the sugar mill's daily operations.

Cate said she imagined a man with a green eyeshade sitting at a tall desk writing each line: purchases of raw materials, capital expenditures for a new piece of equipment or a mule, and receipts from a wholesaler who bought their refined sugar.

He found the payday entries interesting — the lists of names of men and women, their hours and their meager wages. Some got silver coin and others received chits to use at a company store in Thibodaux. Although unrelated to the crimes at Proctor Hall, these books had historic value, and Henri said he'd suggest Doc donate them to the archives in New Orleans.

Once they took the downstairs hallway down to studs, the crew chief moved into the music room opposite the kitchen and began working room by room toward the back of the house. After taking out all the first-floor walls, they'd go upstairs.

Landry showed the trapdoor in the floor to the crew chief, explaining how people sneaked into the house. When it was time to remove the floors, he wanted to examine it. The walls and shelves came down piece by piece, yielding nothing, and the next room was the same.

Last was the sitting room, the one Landry hoped might hold secrets. The floorboards were still brown with bloodstains that had seeped through the carpet when Agnes and Ben positioned the Proctor family's bodies on the couch.

A moment of excitement came when a workman pried away the bookshelf that abutted the fireplace and found a three-foot-wide space that wrapped around the brick flue. Cate was the smallest, and Landry volunteered her to squeeze down the narrow passage and look around the corner behind the chimney.

She coughed as ancient dust flew into her face. "It's empty. No, wait! There's something sitting on a ledge above me. Let me reach…" She raised her arm and closed her fingers around something, pulled it off its resting place, and brought it out.

Cate held a hatchet with a blade as sharp as the day it was finely honed. Dark brown stains covered the steel and the handle.

"We'll check the DNA on it," one of the medical techs said.

Landry said, "My guess is you'll get a mixture of blood samples. The Proctors, Michael and who knows how many others. I'd say you found the murder weapon."

THE PROCTOR HALL HORROR

The work shifted to the second floor. The bedrooms yielded nothing until they reached the final one, May Ellen's haunted room. Only the interior walls were standing, and the room was open to the elements. The work crew installed scaffolds to reach the wall panels and revealed the shaft Julien had told Landry about, so cleverly concealed that no one would have seen it. Agnes had escaped down the ladder inside that narrow passage after decapitating Michael in the bed.

As they worked, everyone experienced an overwhelming feeling of depression. One compared it to being at a funeral — this was a room of sadness and tears. And moments later they discovered why.

A wooden box stood behind each of three wall panels. Julien had said the coffins would be there, but the workers didn't know about them. Even these tough men and women were astonished once they realized what they'd uncovered.

They lowered the boxes to the ground floor with ropes, and the medical team pried up the lid of the smaller box, which held a desiccated corpse packed in lime. "Clothing indicates a female. Her head is missing," one examiner commented.

"May Ellen Proctor," Cate whispered, taking Landry's hand and saying a brief prayer.

That discovery stopped work for the day. The forensic crew loaded the coffins into a van and left for Baton Rouge, and the demolition workers left for the evening as well.

As Landry drove back to New Orleans, he got a call from Lieutenant Kanter. Julien had taken a turn for the worse. He had a temperature of a hundred and five, and the meds to control his skyrocketing blood pressure no longer worked. He was in critical condition, and the next twelve hours would tell the tale for Julien.

BILL THOMPSON

"This morning he handed the nurse a piece of paper — a handwritten will," Kanter advised. "He has no heirs, and he left his possessions to you. He wants to be cremated. The last line says, 'My soul is going to hell anyway, so I might as well let my body burn too.'"

"Bizarre," Landry said, wondering if those stacks of books and papers in his office held more revelations about this man with two lives. Perhaps he'd get to find out.

CHAPTER FIFTY-SEVEN

The next morning Julien Girard died, and Landry wondered what unspoken horrors the man took to the grave with him. Had they only scratched the surface? Now there would be theories and conjectures, but no more validation from one who knew the answers.

The rest of the walls at Proctor Hall came down without incident, and the crew began ripping out floorboards on the ground floor.

Under the floor of the blast-ravaged kitchen, the forensic team found bones that appeared to be human. Instead of inside a coffin, these were half-buried in the dirt.

"Ben Trimble?" Landry asked, and Henri said it matched the story Julien told them.

"Julien said Agnes dragged him under the house and left him for the animals in 2014. I wonder if he was here too. Do you think he might have helped his mother kill his own father?"

Cate said, "I'm sure of it. I wouldn't put anything past these people."

Near the end of the second day, they came across another box that lay under the flooring in the sitting room. It was similar to the ones they'd found upstairs. When the lid was pried up, they found another coffin, but a vastly different burial — a gruesome, unimaginable one.

This time there was no lime packed around the prone, headless body. Before them was a scene of pure horror. The female inside wore overalls and had long blond hair. Her face was contorted into a twisted grimace that even the maggots couldn't erase. Her hands were above her chest, and the fingernails were bloody and jagged. There had been a mighty struggle inside this box.

"Look at the top — there, on the inside," someone said. "Those are claw marks."

"Unbelievable," Landry said. "I think this is Marguey Slattery. Julien said he and Agnes killed her, but he neglected to mention that they buried her alive."

The demo chief said, "I've seen a lot of crazy stuff over the years, but I never imagined turning up bodies in the walls and floors of an old house. Who is that girl?"

Landry explained about Marguey and said the killers were caretakers — Agnes and her son, Julien. The Proctors had been dead for years by then.

The man shook his head in disgust. "What kind of person does that to a girl? You knew the people, right? Were they total psychopaths?"

Landry said, "I never saw the woman. Her son was a university professor for nearly thirty years. He was mild-mannered and friendly. He's that guy you got to know at a

THE PROCTOR HALL HORROR

bar, or the man who drives the streetcar, or the fellow who coaches your kid's team. He's anybody, and he's nobody. You would have never known in a million years what was going on inside his mind."

After the man went back to work, Cate said, "Well, are you glad you got that off your chest? It was like he asked for a street name and you told him how to get to Pittsburgh."

Landry smiled. "I let things build up inside sometimes. I felt sorry for Julien. I believed I knew him, and even when I learned what he was, there were times he seemed to be...maybe remorseful. But was that just a ploy to appear to be like other people?"

"Nobody should feel sorry for him after seeing the girl in the box. What he and his mother did to her is beyond comprehension. He was right — he'll spend eternity in hell. At least I hope so."

They never found Joseph Girard's body. Ben Trimble had said he'd take care of his brother-in-law's corpse, and Landry assumed he buried it somewhere on the property.

Once they finished at the house, everyone left except the wrecking crew. A few days later, a plot of evenly spread dirt marked where Proctor Hall once stood.

Back at home, Cate asked, "What will become of May Ellen and the others? Will their spirits be trapped on the property forever?"

Landry paused and said, "Thanks. You just gave me an idea."

CHAPTER FIFTY-EIGHT

The next morning he called Harry Kanter. "Follow me for a minute on something," he began. "When I first researched Proctor Hall, I found nothing about what happened to the bodies after the massacre. Noah was the rightful heir but also the prime suspect and possibly mentally ill. The cops had three bodies — and three heads — to contend with.

"The torsos ended up in the walls at Proctor Hall. How that happened isn't germane to my question. I want to find out what happened to the heads."

"Good question," Kanter said. "They would have been evidence at first. Somebody would have examined the marks to determine the type of instrument used, taken blood samples, and a million other things. But it would have been the same with the bodies. If the bodies were returned to Proctor Hall, the heads would have gone along with them. Are you certain you all didn't miss them during the demolition?"

"Positive. They aren't there."

Kanter asked why it really mattered after almost sixty years.

"Because I'm going to buy the Proctors caskets and give them a burial in the Thibodaux cemetery. They deserve the respect and to be buried intact. Can you check around to see what might have happened to them?"

Harry said he'd make a call. He knew it would be difficult finding anything about a sixty-year-old cold case, but Landry had a noble goal, and he wanted to help. One thing was certain — the heads were somewhere, and the state medical examiner had the power to find out.

Forty-eight hours later, the man called with an apology. The morgue is a vast place, he said. Things get moved around, and only rarely does something go missing. Sometimes it's the embarrassing moment when a family asks for their loved one's remains.

In 1963 after the medical examiner was finished, the Proctor heads went onto a shelf in one of rows and rows of freezers. They were properly tagged and held awaiting instructions on where to send them. The bodies were much larger and hard to miss, and they went back to Lafourche Parish within months after the deaths.

The heads stayed as new cases arose, and other body parts were stored in front of them. Eventually they were at the rear of a very long shelf that no one ever pulled out all the way. Unfortunately but understandably, they were forgotten.

Two days later a state cop drove a refrigerated van to the funeral home in Thibodaux where the bodies were awaiting burial. An embalmer carefully prepared the heads for interment and the mortuary owner respectfully placed them and their bodies in the caskets Landry and Cate selected. The bodies were complete for the first time in decades. As

THE PROCTOR HALL HORROR

a priest read from the Bible at the graveyard, Landry prayed that they were finally at peace.

The ensuing days were busy for Landry. Jack Blair became his assistant again as Channel Nine's staff put together the new *Bayou Hauntings* episode featuring Proctor Hall. There were production deadlines, interviews with April, Marisol and locals in Thibodaux who related the legends, background footage, hours of voiceovers for Landry and Henri, and a hundred other details required to produce a television documentary.

The assistant professor who took over for Julien gave Marisol and April their well-deserved A grades, and the girls met Landry and Cate for coffee just before leaving New Orleans for the summer. On that day when they chose Proctor Hall as their project, no one could have imagined what sacrifices, heartbreaks and terror they would endure while trying to win a rigged competition.

Days later Cate awoke one morning and began to tell Landry about a dream.

He grinned. "You can stop right there. I had it too."

As it turned out, it was the same for both of them. May Ellen Proctor appeared as a wispy, white phantom, her body now complete. She thanked them for helping her family and her brother Noah. "We can rest now that the house is gone," she said. "I will never forget you." That would be their last contact with the Proctor Hall ghosts.

Landry got a phone call weeks later from Andy Arnaud. He said he'd apologized to everyone else for disappearing, but he just couldn't handle the horror. He worked on an offshore rig in the Gulf where nobody knew him or asked about his experiences. Yes, he still had snow-white hair. He guessed it always would be. He had heard the news about Julien Girard and asked if Marisol and April got their top grade. He promised to check in now and then, but that wouldn't happen. His conversation with Landry only brought up memories he wanted to forget.

Landry and Cate cleaned out Julien's office and moved everything to storage in the building where Henri had his office. Despite being a madman, Julien was a brilliant historian, and his collection of books and papers on Louisiana culture were a treasure trove of information. Landry commented that at least one good thing came from a man whose life was filled with evil.

CHAPTER FIFTY-NINE

Doc Adams moved Noah into one of Houston's premier retirement centers. Money was no object once Doc devised a plan that would set the man up for the rest of his life.

Doc owned Proctor Hall because he'd bought it at a tax sale, but Noah was the last remaining Proctor. Doc believed the thousand-acre plantation should be his. Noah couldn't manage his own finances, so Doc transferred the property to a trust. He and Cate were trustees, and Noah was the beneficiary of the income.

Doc leased half the property to the sugar cooperative and hired a property developer to create a subdivision on the remaining five hundred acres. Within a year there were streets, sewers and utilities, and soon beautiful homes occupied shady ten-acre lots that fronted the bayou.

Every other Sunday, Cate and Landry flew to Houston, met Doc for lunch, and the three of them went to see Noah. They sat in rockers on a shaded veranda and talked about everything from politics to the weather. Noah listened, watched them when they spoke, and Doc said he understood everything they said.

As his primary physician, Doc marveled at how well Noah adapted to a safe, secure environment. When they visited, Noah's caregiver, a middle-aged nurse named Etta Morgan, updated them on his progress.

The kind lady was a blessing to Noah, and she spent untold hours with him. It was Etta who discovered the one thing that made Noah happy — music. She bought him an iPod and headphones and loaded music from every genre. He listened to oldies, pop, Broadway show tunes and, his favorite, classical.

"Watch what happens when he listens," she said one Sunday afternoon. Noah's head moved to the beautiful sounds of his favorite Bach concerto. He tapped his fingers on the chair lightly, and there was the slightest hint of a smile on his face.

On their most recent visit, they brought pizza and root beer, Noah's favorite foods. He ate along with them, obviously enjoying the meal, and when it was time to go, they stood, Cate hugged him, and they told him goodbye.

Noah looked into their eyes and said his first words.

Thank you, friends.

Thank you!

Thanks for reading *The Proctor Hall Horror*.

If you enjoyed it, I'd appreciate a review on Amazon. Reviews are what allow other readers to find books they enjoy, so thanks in advance for your help.

Please join me on:
Facebook
http://on.fb.me/187NRRP
Twitter
@BThompsonBooks

This is book 7 of The Bayou Hauntings Series. The others are available as paperbacks or ebooks.

MAY WE OFFER YOU A FREE BOOK?
Bill Thompson's award-winning first novel,
***The Bethlehem Scroll*, can be yours free.**
Just go to
billthompsonbooks.com
and click
"Subscribe."
Once you're on the list, you'll receive advance notice of future book releases and our newsletter.

Made in United States
Orlando, FL
11 August 2022